A Brief
Moment
in Time

JEANE WATIER

NOVEL *Ink*
PUBLISHING

Library and Archives Canada Cataloguing in Publication
Watier, Jeane, 1963-
A brief Moment in Time / Jeane Watier.
ISBN 978-0-9810703-4-6
I. Title.
PS8645.A846B75 2011   C813'.6   C2011-904918-X

All characters, events, and locations portrayed in this book are fictitious. Any similarity to real persons, places, or events is coincidental and not intended by the author.

Published by: Novel Ink, Calgary, AB
www.novel-ink.com
Cover design and layout by: Serenity Design Concepts
Original artwork/photographs: Billy Frank Alexander (Background: Grunge 5), Cécile Geng (Portrait: woman's face), Gavin Spencer (Beach Romance), Shyle Zacharias (clock), Lynn Cummings (lock and chain), and Ruth Livingstone (Image for chapter headings: keys)

For more information on this book and other books by Jeane Watier go to: **www.jeanewatier.com**

Dedication

To my favorite teachers: Abraham-Hicks, for offering life-changing truths to those ready to hear. Robert Scheinfeld, who embarked on a treasure hunt at a young age, collected the pieces of the puzzle called life, and continues to present them to us in a way that no one has before. Richard Bach, an author who was not afraid to tell stories that are still impacting lives. Wayne Dyer, Ernest Holmes, Louise Hay, and so many others...Thank you for inspiring me!

To my family and friends: your love and encouragement allow me to be all that I can be. Thank you for enriching my life!

Jeane Watier

Prologue

She'd found Gavin just as Kathryn had wanted her to. Now, as Adele listened to him speak, she could feel the depth of emotion he had for her friend. A powerful bond connected the two of them; that was obvious. Still, Adele found it hard to believe. Kathryn and Gavin were strangers; they'd never met—at least not in a way her mind could readily comprehend.

But whether she understood it or not, she couldn't disregard the facts. Kathryn was calling to Gavin Mc-Dermott from another realm, wanting, possibly even needing his help and leaving clues so that Adele could assist her in her quest.

Other realms, parallel realities, paranormal activity—those were topics Adele knew little about, but she'd consulted a friend from college who specialized in such things. He assured her that other realms existed and that comas, hallucinations, sleep, even daydreaming, drew people into those realms temporarily, although much of it remained in the subconscious. He explained that the shift in focus could be powerful enough to impress itself in a person's conscious memory, as in Gavin's experience. And in Kathryn's case, he believed that what she was experiencing was so "real" it had the power to hold her in the other realm. Furthermore, he'd confirmed Adele's belief that a visit from Gavin could be the impetus needed to draw Kathryn from the comatose state she was in.

Now Adele had to get him there, but it wasn't going to be easy; plenty of obstacles stood in the way. And time, as she knew it, was running out.

Part 1

~Gavin~

There is a fine line between dreams and reality;
it's up to you to draw it.

—B. QUILLIAM

Chapter 1

"It's a system, kid. You learn the system and you'll do just fine." Gavin remembered the words as if they'd been spoken yesterday. In reality, it was seventeen years ago.

As he watched the new inmate, Gavin felt sorry for him. The boy had to be eighteen, although he didn't look it. He'd no doubt have it hard for the first while, but he'd get used to it; he really didn't have a choice. He had some sense to him, however, staring straight ahead, not looking at anyone, his face not portraying the emotions he must be feeling.

He continued that way until nearly across the big yard, then for some reason turned to look at Gavin. The boy was a hundred feet away, but Gavin could see into his eyes and for a moment into his very soul. It was like looking at himself seventeen years earlier: a scared kid, tall but scrawny, feeling that his life was over—or wishing it was—all because of one regrettable night, one very stupid decision.

The brief eye contact and sudden onslaught of memories that accompanied it left Gavin unsettled. *Why did he look at me like that? It almost seemed like he did it on purpose...like he knew me or something.* Gavin was curious now. He wondered what the kid was in for. It had to be serious; Swenton was a maximum-security prison.

Gavin had been the topic of conversation himself, so young and naive all those years ago. The nickname he'd received, Babyface McDermott, reflected that. Anyone who knew him now, however, called him Gavin to his face.

Nearly everybody had nicknames in the joint, and Gavin didn't really mind his. Somehow he'd gained a tough reputation despite or maybe because of the nickname; he wasn't sure. At six foot four, two hundred thirty pounds, nobody messed with him anymore.

Anyone who'd been in prison awhile knew how to present himself to a first timer, or fish, as they were called. It was a game they played—forming allies, choosing friends carefully, spreading rumors. Gavin just shook his head at some of those rumors. They were ridiculous at best, but the fish didn't know that. He'd supposedly killed two fellow convicts. His hands, it was said, were lethal weapons, and a blow to the head in just the right spot would kill a man instantly.

Gavin played their game; it was a game of survival, but he wasn't that person. In the first year of his prison term, he'd made the decision to take advantage of the programs offered and become all that he could be. He couldn't change that unfortunate night; he couldn't go back and undo what he'd done, but he could move forward. He could change himself.

And he *had* changed—inwardly. But on the outside, he played his role. The only time he let his defenses down was at night when alone in his cell. There he would retreat into the world he had created, a world that had kept him sane all those years. In his own private domain he could be the person he wanted to be, the person he was underneath. He could dream and imagine. He could escape.

The dinner bell sounded, jarring Gavin from his uncharacteristic daydream. He looked around quickly to ensure that no one had caught him staring into space. Despite his tough reputation, he still kept himself guarded around the other convicts. The men didn't take kindly to change, and strange behavior simply wasn't tolerated.

He saw what had happened to Arthur Talon. Dubbed "Mr. T," the guy was well respected by most of the men, but things changed. Arthur found religion, which wasn't that uncommon in the joint, but in his zeal for the Lord, he made some enemies. What started as a mealtime joke turned into a campaign to put a stop to his "holier than thou" behavior. He took it all piously, believing it was his cross to bear, but it became so bad that he was beaten to within an inch of his life, and after that he was transferred out.

The prisoners filed mindlessly to the dining hall. There was a system in place there too, an unwritten code dictating who sat where and with whom. It was dutifully followed day in and day out, nobody thinking to question a system that had been in place from the start.

As Gavin waited in line, he watched the new kid. He was six or seven men ahead of him, and Gavin could observe him without drawing attention to himself. As he filled his tray, he noticed the kid sitting alone. Everybody was avoiding him. It was typical treatment of a first timer.

Then Gavin did something that surprised even himself. He turned to Stubby, in line behind him, and explained, "I'm gonna see what I can find out." He walked over to the new kid and without a word, sat across the table from him. Gavin was aware that the whole room had turned to watch, but it was too late to change his mind. He would have to deal with the consequences, whatever they might be.

The two ate in silence for a moment, not looking at anything but the food in front of them. Gavin was deciding what to say to the kid, how to question him while still playing the game. He was surprised when the boy was the first to speak.

"I'm Ryan."

"Gavin." As he mumbled his reply, he met the boy's eyes and again saw something familiar. He was quick to dismiss it, but he couldn't disregard the look on the boy's face; it didn't match his circumstances. The kid didn't seem afraid, and it unnerved Gavin.

"I know who you are."

A silent alarm went off in Gavin's head as he heard the calm declaration. Outwardly, he showed no evidence of it; he had trained himself well. Even so, his mind was scrambling. *What did the kid mean by that? Has he heard things about me in the few short days he's been here, or did he hear about me on the outside?*

Those questions brought up an issue Gavin had been grappling with in recent months. With his prison term nearing an end, he'd begun speculating what it would be like when he got out and what others would know and say about him. He'd asked his parents more than once, his sister too, but they were biased. They'd continued to love and support him all those years. His family didn't see him as a murderer or even a criminal for that matter, but that didn't change the facts, and it didn't determine how others would see him.

He let the comment go by without as much as a raised eyebrow. He had to play the kid. He had to stay in control of the conversation and defend his reputation. That, he knew for sure.

Ryan didn't seem intimidated by him. He was very composed for someone so young and, Gavin could only assume, out of his element.

"You're Gavin McDermott. I know who you are," he repeated. "I'm from Redding."

Redding was just twenty miles from Gavin's home. It was also where he'd gone to high school and where he'd been on that ill-fated night. Now the kid had the upper hand, and Gavin had to ask, "What's your last name?"

"Terley."

Gavin's blood went cold. He knew the name all too well. More questions begged to be asked, but Gavin managed to keep his composure. He wanted to know who the kid's parents were, what crime he'd committed to get himself incarcerated at Swenton, and most of all, what he knew about him.

At one time, Redding had been a thriving town with a population of about ten thousand. A lumber mill employed many of the town's residents, but when the mill shut down, hard times followed and crime increased. Gangs were common in Gavin's school, and it was a run-in with a gang that changed his life forever.

And the name, Terley—it was the same last name as the kid Gavin had been charged with killing. He wondered if Ryan was related and how much he knew of the details of that night.

"So, what did you do to get in here?" Gavin asked as dispassionately as he could.

The kid looked at him for a moment before he answered evenly, "I killed my stepfather." It was a blunt admission of guilt, and Gavin grimaced inwardly, knowing there was much more to the story. He nodded and continued eating, as if hearing that kind of statement was commonplace. The truth was, he had never gotten used to it. Hearing about a murder only served to remind him of his own experience and fill him with the sickening dread he'd felt when it happened.

They were nearly done eating, and very few words had passed between them, but Gavin had a plan in mind.

He needed to know what the kid knew about him, and for that information, he was willing to make a deal.

"Listen, I don't know what it is you've heard about me, kid." Gavin kept his voice low and even, making it sound as threatening as he could. "But in here I decide what people say about me and what they don't. Is that understood?"

Ryan nodded, still no fear in his eyes. The boy wasn't more than a hundred and forty pounds; he even had a kind of frailty about him, yet he wasn't afraid. It didn't seem right to Gavin.

"I'm going to do something for you," he informed the kid. "In exchange for you keeping your mouth shut, I'm gonna save you some pain."

The boy frowned slightly, obviously not understanding but not betraying his calm facade to the others watching.

"I'm going to spread a story about you to the other men," Gavin stated. "It'll keep a few of the trouble-makers away. Your job is to dummy up. People question you, you don't admit anything; you don't deny anything. Agreed?"

The kid nodded a second time as Gavin got up from the table, took his tray to the counter, and then walked out of the dining hall, aware again that all eyes were on him.

Stubby caught up to him as he walked down the hallway. As the name implied, the man was short and stocky; nevertheless, he was a force to be reckoned with if he got angry. Stubby had been in Swenton nearly as long as Gavin, and the two had become friends early on.

"So?"

Gavin hadn't completely settled on just how he would weave the story about Ryan, but he had some ideas and knew he had to go with them. Friend or not, Stubby had to be an unwitting accomplice in order for his little scheme to work.

"The kid's psycho." Gavin threw out some bait.

"Really? What did he say?" Stubby liked a good bit of gossip as well as the next guy, and Gavin knew he had him.

"It wasn't so much what he said," Gavin explained, "as what he didn't say. The kid was cool as a cucumber, and when I looked him in the eye..." Gavin stopped and shuddered, adding conviction to his words. "I could have been looking at a young Hannibal Lecter."

"You don't say," Stubby replied, transfixed. "What did he do?"

"Killed his father." Gavin altered the truth slightly to provide more drama. For the clincher he added, "Mother died mysteriously awhile back, too. And when he told me it...his eyes...I couldn't even look straight at him. There's something really disturbing about him."

That was all Gavin needed to say. The story was good. Stubby had bought it without question and would take it from there. By noon the next day, the whole place would know that the new fish was a cross between Damien Thorn, Hannibal Lecter, and the devil himself. Nevertheless, it left Gavin with a dilemma. He wanted to talk to the kid more and find out what he knew about him.

The men played basketball in the big yard after dinner, and Stubby was the first to notice that the kid was watching them. "Why's he looking at us like that? It's kind of creepy, don't you think?"

"Yeah, it is," Gavin played along. "I hope I didn't piss him off before. Maybe I should try to do something to get on his good side. Why don't I ask him if he wants to join us for a game?"

Stubby shook his head adamantly. "Don't rope me into this. I don't want to have anything to do with the little shit."

"Well, I gotta try something." With that, Gavin walked over to where the boy was standing.

"It's done," he announced simply. "All kinds of stories will be circulating about you by tomorrow. You up for your end of the deal?"

"Yeah."

The two men stood silently for a few minutes, hands in their pockets, kicking at the gravel beneath their feet. Finally Gavin had to ask, "So what did you hear about me?"

The kid continued looking down for a moment longer and then replied without emotion, "You killed my father."

Chapter 2

A blade of cold, piercing steel thrust itself into Gavin's chest as he heard the boy's words. A chill ran through him, and for a moment he was almost tempted to believe the dark rumors he'd started about the kid. Knife still twisting inside, Gavin continued looking down, rearranging the pebbles beneath him with the toe of his shoe.

"I never knew him, of course, but my mom talked about him," Ryan explained.

Gavin couldn't see any other course of action than to stand and listen to the boy talk. He wanted to walk away—run away, make the kid stop—but he'd been the one to ask the question, and now he sincerely regretted it.

"She hated him."

The words caused Gavin's head to jerk upward, his eyes focusing in on the boy's face.

"He used her until she got pregnant with me. She was only fifteen at the time.

"Mom raised me on her own," Ryan continued, his face devoid of emotion. "A few years ago, she got married. The guy started beating her. I warned him to stop, but he just laughed at me." The kid's face held no remorse as he summed up the story. "So I had to make him stop."

Inwardly, Gavin reacted to the kid's blunt declaration. *No remorse, no regret, no fear; how can he not show any emotion? From the sounds of it, he committed a premeditated, cold-blooded murder. And now he's undoubtedly facing life in prison. How can he be so calm about it?*

He couldn't even come up with an appropriate response. The kid had obviously had a rough life. He'd undoubtedly learned to shut off his emotions as a survival mechanism. Yet somehow Gavin sensed it was more than that, but he couldn't for the life of him figure out what it might be or why he felt drawn to the mysterious young man.

As he looked around them, he noticed others glance in their direction and then turn away just as quickly, but nobody came near.

"Look," Gavin said finally. "About our deal. This'll work if you keep quiet. But if you do run into any trouble..."

"It's okay. I can take care of myself." The kid's words sounded convincing, not like some smart ass with more brawn than brains, but rather like someone who'd been taking care of himself for a long time, someone who knew what he was talking about.

Gavin started to leave, then turned back to Ryan with what he hoped sounded like a threat. "It helps to know who your friends are in here."

The kid nodded.

Gavin walked away maintaining an outward calm, yet silently imploding. He gave Stubby a look that said, "The kid's even more messed than I thought," and then continued past him, leaving his friend to draw his own conclusions.

Alone in his cell, Gavin sought refuge in the private world he had created. It was a world he could usually escape to with ease; he'd been doing it for so many years. But that evening, Ryan's words haunted his familiar place.

The demons of his own past haunted him, too. Though he'd worked hard to bury them, he'd obviously been unsuccessful. He fell into a fitful sleep. He was eighteen again, filled with hope for the future. Yet when he looked in a mirror, it was Ryan's image, not his own, that stared back at him. And when he looked down, there was blood on his hands.

Strict routine ruled the lives of the prisoners at Swenton. The morning bell sounded, bringing them back to the harsh reality of their incarcerated world. For once, Gavin was glad to re-enter that world. The one he'd just experienced in his dreams was a greater hell by far. He'd awoken in a sweat, having run from something much too frightening to remember.

At breakfast, announcements were made for the day. A rehabilitation program was being initiated at Swenton. Prisoners within two years of their parole were being "encouraged" to attend. Incentives were being offered to those willing to participate in the program. What it boiled down to in Gavin's mind was that those who didn't attend would have to work longer hours. It didn't sound like incentive to him, just another form of coercion.

The program began that morning with nearly forty in attendance in the prison auditorium. The men around Gavin were whispering about the so-called rehabilitation being offered. He heard the usual scoffing, some obviously against the idea, others asking questions. The room went silent, however, as a woman walked onto the stage.

She was fortyish, Gavin guessed, and not unattractive—just somewhat plain looking with her hair pulled back a little too severely in a bun. She might have had a decent figure as well, but it was covered in a coat-style dress that gave very little indication of what was underneath.

Nevertheless, judging by the men's response, she may as well have been Madonna. Gavin noticed her blush slightly as she cleared her throat to begin.

Speaking loudly over the still-audible whistle, jeer, or muffled comment, the woman introduced herself as Kathryn Harding. She then listed her qualifications, to which Gavin didn't really listen; he was much more interested in the conversations going on around him.

She'll have her work cut out, he mused. *No one's taking her seriously.*

As she continued, a few words and phrases caught Gavin's interest. Others around him must have heard too, because the room became quiet.

"This is an innovative approach," she was saying, "developed by some of the leading psychologists in the country. With this methodology we don't use labels, except to say that we're all teachers and all students. There is no therapist or patient. No murderer, no criminal, no victim. We are all equal—human beings who have chosen different experiences in life.

"Our goal will be to help you see yourself free of those labels. And once free of them, you can begin to see yourself as anything you want to be."

Gavin was riveted to her words. They were completely different from what he'd been expecting, and they affected him deeply. He felt torn. He wanted to dismiss them as outlandish, impossible even, yet part of him wanted to believe they were true. Commonsense argued that it wouldn't matter how he saw himself; people would always look at what he had done and label him as a murderer. He could hide from it. He could pretend otherwise, but he couldn't change what was.

She went on to describe the program, which consisted of group sessions and individual counseling. In addition, she would be choosing four to six men to work with for an extended period, those particular men being chosen according to the proximity of their parole, their record of behavior, and their participation in the group and individual sessions. Her plan was to continue to work with those men once they were fully released.

Gavin wasn't sure why, when he had serious doubts about the validity of the woman's claims, but for some reason he wanted to be a part of her little experimental group. Moreover, he sensed he would be.

The woman introduced her colleagues, two men and another woman who would be working with her in the program. Sessions would be starting the following week, and groups and times would be posted in the dining hall.

The prisoners, glad to have missed an hour of work, were dismissed to go to their jobs. Gavin listened to the chatter as the men made their way to the industry area. Some were still making crude jokes about the women they had just seen, while others challenged the effectiveness of the rehabilitation program.

Gavin was caught up in his own introspection—a mixture of thoughts and feelings composed of Ryan's words, his own unsettling dream, and the strange, enticing things the woman had just shared.

"The only thing I need to rehabilitate me," Stubby interjected, "is a good woman and a place to call home when I get out of this shit hole."

Several others agreed by nodding or grunting. Although somewhat primal, Gavin couldn't disagree with the sentiment. Stubby, along with many of the other inmates Gavin had gotten to know, had learned their lesson. They wouldn't be repeating their crime. In a sense, they were already rehabilitated. They were not the same men they'd been ten or twenty years before.

Gavin wasn't either. He hardly knew the foolish kid he'd been seventeen years earlier. That kid was long gone—or at least he'd thought so—until he'd met Ryan, until that dream had made it all seem so real again.

As he entered the millwork shop where he worked as a supervisor, the first face to greet him was none other than Ryan's. The kid half smiled and shrugged his shoulders. "They told me to report here. What do you want me to do?"

Gavin quickly assessed the situation. Jobs were assigned according to seniority. He pretty much ran the place now and had men he trusted working the big machines. Fish were usually a pain in the ass, and more often than not they liked to complain rather than work. The work wasn't complicated, but a stupid or careless move could cost someone a finger or an arm.

He sighed. With little choice in the matter, he gave Ryan some simple instructions and had him work with Rocco. Then he went over to the other side of the room where one of the planers was acting up. He knew it so well, he could repair it with his eyes closed.

As he worked, his thoughts fixated on the woman they'd just heard. *Does she really believe that we're all the same? Does she honestly see herself as equal to the men she just addressed?* He questioned again what the benefit of that kind of reasoning would be. *Is it for real or just some new psychological trickery, a way to mess with our minds?*

Gavin believed the mind was a complicated thing, capable of more than most people believed. He'd proved it over the years. He could escape in his mind when he was alone at night. He'd honed it well, but he'd never spoken of it to anyone, not even his family who visited him regularly.

He wondered what this woman's view might be on subjects like that. He doubted it was something he'd ever be comfortable sharing, but still he was curious.

Gavin looked up to see Rocco walking toward him with a scowl on his face.

"I can't work with the kid, Gavin. I don't know if you've heard the rumors, but I've heard some pretty wild stuff about him. I believe it, too. You just have to look at his eyes—something about him is really disturbing."

Gavin coughed to keep from laughing as he listened to the older man's concerns. Rocco was a friend of Stubby's and as superstitious as they come. Gavin's plan was going smoothly.

"All right, send him over here."

Ryan appeared minutes later, and Gavin put him to work tightening some bolts on the planer. After a few minutes of silence, he hoped the kid would be content with the lack of communication, but it didn't last.

"How long till you get out?"

"A year, maybe longer." Gavin was eligible for parole within the year, but most were denied the first time, and he didn't want to get his hopes up.

"What are you gonna do?"

"Don't know yet," Gavin shrugged.

"What's that rehab program all about?"

"I guess they want to try and make respectable citizens out of us."

"We're no different than they are."

Gavin stared at the kid. The statement came out of nowhere, yet it was oddly similar to the one the psychologist woman had made earlier. Again it wasn't so much from a place of defiance as a place of knowing. He wondered what made the kid tick, how his mind worked.

"Why do you say that?" Gavin asked.

"It's who we all are, deep down. You, me, that guard." Ryan motioned ever so slightly with his head. "We're all the same."

"In what way?"

"What we're made of, what we're capable of…None of this is real, you know."

Chapter 3

Again, Gavin woke up in a panic, drenched in sweat as the morning bell sounded. It was becoming an uncomfortable pattern—one that he longed to change.

He'd been attending the group sessions three times a week for two weeks already, and individual sessions were scheduled to start that morning. The woman that had introduced the program was the facilitator of his group, but she was different from the woman who'd spoken in the assembly that first morning. She seemed more relaxed as she got to know the men, and as she loosened up, she let more of her personality show. Gavin was truly enjoying the meetings and was looking forward to the individual sessions.

She led the group in a guided meditation at the start of each meeting. At first the men found it a joke, and when instructed to focus on something enjoyable, all kinds of crude suggestions were offered.

By the end of the second week Kate, as she'd asked the men to call her, was making progress. Gavin found the exercise easy enough, but kept most of his thoughts to himself. It was very similar to the mind games he played, or used to play, at night. The now-frequent nightmares had all but obliterated the refuge he'd created. Something about Ryan's presence, and now Kate's, had changed things, complicated things, in his life.

Kate had them close their eyes and try to imagine a space. She helped them define it, making it their own. Then each time they would return to their space, but they would embellish it, notice or create something new within it. She repeatedly told them the space was theirs alone, that it was a safe place that no one else could enter without their permission. She encouraged them to make it personal with images of loved ones, to fill it with objects and activities that interested them. It was their haven, a space uniquely theirs that no one could take away, change, or destroy.

Gavin was amazed that he could, even in the presence of Kate and nine other men, enter his space and become so caught up in it that he was unaware of anything else happening. It was like some sort of hypnotism.

Each time the men sat in a circle, facing outward, and Kate walked around the perimeter, talking in a soothing voice, guiding each to his own personal sanctuary. Mystical music played softly in the background, and Gavin could picture a robed man in the swaying grasses of a far-off land, playing his flute by a bubbling stream while birds called out their greetings. It was easy to be drawn away to a better place.

After meditating for about fifteen minutes, Kate spoke to the group, and then they participated in a question and answer period. Gavin hung on her words, and as the days progressed, he had more and more questions that he couldn't bring himself to ask. He hoped he'd feel more comfortable during the individual counseling.

Gavin entered the designated room when it was time for his private session, and Kate greeted him with a smile. He couldn't help but notice that she had an attractive quality about her. She still wore her hair in a bun and dressed a little too conservatively for her age, but her eyes were bright, and her kind smile made Gavin feel at ease.

"Hello, Gavin," she said in the soft, silvery voice that he had come to know from their group sessions. "Have a seat."

"Thanks."

A large desk was the focal point of the room, but Kate didn't sit behind it. She sat in one of two identical chairs positioned in the center of the small room. The lighting was subtle—just a dim lamp on the desk and some natural light coming in through vertical blinds.

"Have you been enjoying our sessions?"

"Yeah, I have," Gavin replied sincerely. "It's nice of you to help us escape like that."

She smiled at his play on words. "It's something you can do yourself now that you know how. You can go to your special place any time you like."

Gavin wanted to share his experiences but felt some lingering apprehension. Instead, he just nodded.

"What I want to convey in these sessions is an understanding of who you are. How would you describe yourself, Gavin?"

Gavin knew she'd have background information on the prisoners she was counseling, but he was candid anyway. "I'm a convicted felon, serving time for second-degree murder."

"Is that all you are?"

Gavin shrugged. "In here it is."

She gently corrected him. "You're still a son, even though you're in prison. Isn't that right?"

Gavin nodded.

"You're a brother, a friend, a citizen of this country? What about the work you do every day? Aren't you a supervisor?" She glanced at her notes.

He nodded again, beginning to understand where she was leading.

"Those are labels our society has given you, Gavin, and they all define you in some way or another." She handed him a sheet of paper with several columns of words on it. "I want you to look at these words and circle the ones that you think describe you best."

Gavin took the pen that she offered and glanced at the page. It was an extensive collection of adjectives in alphabetical order from "able" to "zealous." As he stared at the intimidating list, Kate offered encouragement. "Nobody else gets to see this, and there's no right or wrong. It's just a starting place to help me know how you see yourself."

Gavin circled half a dozen words, trying to be as honest as he could in describing himself. He handed the paper back to Kate.

"Now..." She handed him another paper identical to the first. "I want you to circle words that you think others might use to describe you."

Gavin grimaced, not liking the second exercise. His parents had been nothing but supportive. He had the respect of many of the other convicts and even some of the guards. But when he heard the word *others*, he thought of the world in general and felt as if "murderer" was tattooed across his forehead for all to see. He looked up at Kate.

She was patiently waiting for him to complete the exercise. "It's not as easy, is it?"

"No," Gavin sighed.

"That's fine, let's move on. Why don't you circle words you'd *like* people to use to describe you?"

She must have seen the hesitation that was still evident on Gavin's face, because she changed her tactic. "Okay, how about this? I want you to imagine that you've just come to this planet. Nobody knows you, and you have no past. You're a brand new person, ready to make a brand new life for yourself. The words that you choose to define yourself are exactly what you'll become."

"That's easier," Gavin admitted, liking the world of make-believe that Kate offered but questioning it just the same.

Kate looked at the list Gavin handed her. She smiled. "This is the Gavin McDermott I see before me." She read the words aloud. "You already are all these things, Gavin. Do you believe that?"

"No," he admitted. "Not really."

"This is going to be our work together. For the next few weeks, I'm going to help you see that who you are is not what you think about yourself. It's not what others think of you. Who you are is something fundamental and unchanging. It's the basis of who we all are. We're the same, Gavin. You and me. You just don't know it yet."

Gavin left the meeting uplifted. Being around Kate left him feeling like a normal human being. He almost did feel like her equal when he was with her. He still didn't understand how others would be able to see it that way, but it was a start, something he truly enjoyed.

With a little work, he'd managed to avoid conversations with Ryan, and that helped his over-all state of mind as well. He found the kid peculiar, making him uneasy and, oddly enough, curious at the same time. What was really strange was that some of the things the boy said seemed to reiterate the ideas Kate was introducing.

The next morning, however, after listening to complaints about the kid, who'd received the nickname "Chucky," Gavin had no choice but to put Ryan to work with him.

"I might have spread it on a bit too thick, telling those stories about you," Gavin admitted. "Now nobody wants to have anything to do with you."

"It's the way I wanted it."

Gavin frowned. *The kid actually believes he's responsible for the situation turning out the way it did, like he's controlling the events of his life, somehow? If he truly believes that, then what the hell is he doing in prison?*

"This isn't real, you know," Ryan repeated the strange words he'd spoken once before. "You, me, this place—none of it's real."

He was sure now that Ryan wasn't playing with a full deck, and Gavin was suddenly thankful for the rumors he'd started about him. It served to keep the kid quiet. If the others discovered what he really believed, if they heard him talking this nonsense, they'd know he was really just crazy, delusional, and they'd have him for lunch. He decided to humor the kid. "Okay, we're not real; this place isn't real. What are we doing here then?"

"You could be anywhere you want, tell any story you want. You get stuck sometimes, though, believing you can't leave. The prison is really in your mind."

"Well then, my mind is a powerful thing, kid," Gavin replied sarcastically.

Ryan looked at him and nodded as if acknowledging the great truth he'd just spoken. Strangely enough Gavin felt it, too. Only now he was more confused than ever. He was glad when the lunch bell sounded, ending the conversation. He turned off the machine they were working on and walked away.

Gavin was surprised that the other men didn't discuss the counseling sessions they were attending. He quietly listened to the usual banter around the lunch table, not feeling inclined to bring up the sessions, either. He was enjoying them for reasons he couldn't explain, and he knew if they became a topic at mealtime they'd be reduced to a joke, with Kate and the other counselors at the center of it.

He liked Kate. He respected her. If he was honest, he'd even have to admit he was somewhat attracted to her. He'd barely seen a woman in seventeen years, never mind spending time alone with one, and Kate made him feel good about himself. He looked forward to their sessions.

A little crush on my therapist isn't a bad thing, he decided. *It's probably even normal.*

He wasn't crazy; he wouldn't let it get out of control. He knew he'd never act on it, as it was purely one-sided. She was a professional, an older woman—and a married one at that. Gavin couldn't help but notice the rings on her left hand.

At their next session, Gavin observed something different about Kate. Her hair was up, but it was looser, more attractive, and although she was still dressed conservatively, her outfit was more fashionable, making her look quite becoming. She even had a touch of eye makeup on.

She must have noticed the look he gave her, because she explained, "I'm meeting with representatives from the university right after our session. They want me to update them on the progress we're making with the program here."

"So you are making progress?" he asked, wanting to engage in conversation. He was curious to know more about the woman.

"Yes," she smiled. "I have some very favorable results to show them."

Gavin wondered what she meant by favorable. He also wondered what she thought of his progress and if he would be regarded as a candidate for her ongoing program.

She was polite, but their time was limited so she got right down to business. "Gavin, today I'd like us to start with a guided meditation. Are you okay with that?"

"Sure," he shrugged. He enjoyed the meditations they did in the group and liked hearing the sound of her voice.

She walked over and completely closed the blinds on the window, blanketing the room in shadows. Then she turned on a CD player, and gentle, flowing music filled the room. It had a pleasing tone to it. She instructed him to close his eyes and take several deep breaths to relax.

"Gavin," she began in her silky-smooth tone. "I want you to imagine yourself in your special place. It's a warm, cozy space where you're safe, where you can relax and be yourself," she reminded him softly. "This space belongs to you alone." She paused, and Gavin let himself be drawn into the make-believe world.

"You're completely comfortable and secure in your space, but you're curious now. You want to expand, to explore this new world of yours. You stand up, and as you move forward, your space moves and expands with you.

"As you look into the distance, you see a beach with golden sand along a pristine lake. The water is as bright an emerald green as you've ever seen. It's enticing, and as you begin to think about it, you're right there. Time and distance don't exist in your space, Gavin, only thought." Again, she paused to let Gavin take in his new surroundings.

"You slip off your shoes and feel the warm sand squishing between your toes. As you step into the sparkling water, the refreshing coolness splashes your legs. You shed your outer clothes and dive in. You're a powerful swimmer, and your body slices across the sun-warmed lake." As she let the words sink in again, Gavin could feel the forward movement of his body in the water.

"You're enjoying the delicious freedom of movement, but now you begin to relax in the gentle waves and let them carry you away…"

Mesmerized by her words, Gavin felt his body leaning. He was relaxed, but he trusted the chair to support him. He was so completely caught up in the rapturous sound of Kate's voice and the titillating world into which she was leading him, that he began to disconnect from his physical body.

With her voice and her presence powerfully influencing his voyage, he welcomed her into his imaginary world. It seemed right that she should be with him enjoying the place they had created. As they walked together on the beach, she reached for his hand, and he turned to her, surprised. Her hair fell past her shoulders and flowed freely in the breeze. Her skin was bronze from the sun and her cheeks rosy. Her lips looked soft and inviting. Gavin couldn't resist; he kissed her, and she responded as if it was the most natural thing in the world.

Suddenly she laughed and ran ahead, teasing, beckoning him to follow. Then, instead of running on the beach, they were on horseback. They rode side by side on the endless beach, laughing at the pleasure of it as the breeze caressed their faces.

"Feel the wind in your hair, Gavin," Kate's lulling voice continued. "Now look down. See the emerald lake below. See the lush hillsides and the pastures. Feel your body as it catches the current and rises with it. Now let yourself fall, and feel the rush as you dive down, down, and then up again. Let the current carry you. Let it take you wherever you want to go."

Gavin was marginally aware that he was sliding down in the chair, his body completely limp. At the same time he was soaring high in the sky, caring little about what was happening in the physical shell he'd left behind.

"Now you're standing in a sun-drenched meadow with daisies all around you. The smell of clover is thick in the air. You breathe in the intoxicating smells and feel the velvety rays on your face. As you sit in the tall, flowing grass, a warmth gathers around you. It's a familiar warmth. It's your space, Gavin. Your comfortable, personal space.

"Take a deep breath now, and feel immense appreciation for this space of yours. You know you can return any time you like and have any adventure you want. It's okay to leave it; you know you'll return soon." She paused and then said softly, "You can open your eyes now, Gavin."

Gavin opened his eyes to see her sitting in the chair across from him, clipboard and pen in hand as if she'd been taking notes. Gavin was suddenly conscious of the fact that he was halfway out of his chair, and he quickly pulled himself upright.

"Did you enjoy that?" she asked.

"Mmm," he nodded in response, not sure that he was even capable of words at that moment. He had no idea what had just happened. Whatever it was, it felt real, as if he had actually experienced it—even the kiss. His lips were still tingling. He really hoped that Kate wouldn't ask him to describe the details of his adventure, because her being with him had been purely his creation, not hers.

It was far beyond what he'd experienced in the group sessions or alone in his cell at night. He could go places in his imagination and enjoy the feeling of being somewhere else, but never had he felt the rich, visceral sensations he'd just experienced.

He needed to know. "Was that an out-of-body experience?"

"Is that what it felt like?"

"Yeah," he nodded. "I think so."

"Good," she smiled. "You looked like you'd gone somewhere. Your body nearly slithered off the chair like it was an empty shell. Most people don't have such a complete withdrawal of consciousness their first time. Have you ever done this before?"

"At night, sometimes, I like to escape," Gavin admitted. "But I've never felt so completely gone."

"It was probably just the next step for you, then."

"How does it work?"

"It's really quite simple. We're consciousness focused in a physical body. Most of us spend our lives so completely focused in this way that we think this body is the sum of all that we are. We believe that we begin at birth and end at death."

Gavin glanced at her to make sure she wasn't joking. Her face told him she was serious, although her eyes had a sparkle he hadn't noticed before.

"We're eternal beings, Gavin."

He loved hearing her say his name. It was like a gentle caress each time she said it.

"You're more than this physical body. You just experienced it."

The look on his face must have told her he wasn't quite convinced, so she continued. "Think of the ocean, Gavin. Our physical bodies are like individual drops of water, but at the same time we're part of something infinitely bigger. There's no separation; we have all the qualities and characteristics of the ocean we're a part of, and if we start to really examine ourselves we can't see where we end and where the ocean begins.

"Only instead of water, it's an ocean of energy we exist in. It's conscious and alive, pure and complete. Everything is made up of this energy, Gavin…you and

I and everyone else are a part of it. That's what I meant when I said we're all the same."

She stopped talking, allowing Gavin time to absorb what she'd just said.

He had a question burning in his mind, and although he was trying to resist it, arguing that it was really stupid, he couldn't. "Are we real, then? Is anything real?"

"Reality is…a tricky thing," Kate replied, the sparkle in her eyes hinting at so much more.

The clock on the wall indicated that their time was up, but he still had dozens of questions.

"We'll talk more about this next time," she assured him. "Keep practicing. I want you to trust your space, let it take you anywhere you want to go. Remember, Gavin, nothing is wrong or off limits or inappropriate."

As she added the last statement, Gavin wondered if she suspected something, if she knew somehow that his adventure had gone beyond the words she'd offered as guidance, that he'd embellished the meditation with thoughts of her.

Chapter 4

Gavin awoke to the sound of a gunshot. He bolted upright, his heart pounding and hands shaking as he gripped the sides of his cot. Looking around his familiar cell, lit only by the dim lighting in the corridor, he breathed heavily, still on edge but relieved to be free from his terrifying dream.

Suddenly he longed for Kate's soothing voice. He wanted to escape with her on one of their adventures. She'd said it was something he could do anytime. He'd tried, but it didn't feel the same without her leading.

In the darkness, he tried to imagine her voice and picture the places she had shown him in their sessions together. She was always with him in his mind as he explored his imaginary world. They'd flown a biplane, ridden camels in the desert, and sailed the ocean. They'd climbed mountains and swam in placid lakes. They had sat together watching a brilliant, fiery sunset and had spent evenings on a deserted beach watching the stars.

And they'd kissed. Nothing more—just the exquisite thrill of a first kiss every time they were together.

Gavin knew he was limiting it to that. He knew that to allow it to become more would be to cross a forbidden boundary, yet something inside told him it could be so much more.

Thoughts of Kate helped diminish the gut-wrenching panic that had woken him. The panic was happening regularly now, and he had yet to share it with her in their sessions. He wanted to—now more then ever. The nightmares were accelerating in both frequency and intensity, and keeping them to himself was nearly unbearable.

He was scheduled to have a session that morning, but it was several long hours away, and he didn't dare fall back asleep, to be drawn into the gripping horror again. Instead, he leaned against the cold, bare wall beside his cot and took a few deep breaths. Kate always instructed the men to breathe deeply before a guided meditation. Gavin hadn't understood the significance of it, but now as he breathed in with thoughts of Kate active in his mind, he felt her. A warm presence hovered near him, but he didn't dare open his eyes. He wanted to go wherever the presence would lead him.

He continued to breathe consciously and keep his thoughts focused on Kate. He could see her in his mind, and he carefully went over every detail—the way he saw her in their adventures together.

Unlike her more conservative physical counterpart, the Kate of his dreams wore her hair down. Always smiling or laughing, she was adorned in bright, colorful clothing—loose flowing fabrics wrapped around her beautiful body, covering and yet revealing. She was always calling to him or taking him by the hand, leading him on enticing adventures.

With Kate, he was free. With her, he could be anyone or anything he wanted to be. She was his salvation, his angel, his guide. She was loving and encouraging, never judging, never correcting.

His heart soared as he thought of her. Appreciation filled his heart. Whether in person as his counselor, or in spirit as his adventure-mate and guide, he owed her so much. She had shown him a new world—one he had barely begun to explore.

He had many questions to ask her, but he'd held back, not wanting to let slip the way he'd come to feel about her, not wanting to admit that she was such a vital part of his fantasy world.

Feeling her comforting presence with him in the darkness, he dared ask the questions on his mind, questions he couldn't ask her physical equivalent.

Who are you, Kate?

"I represent all you are and all you desire to be."

Gavin heard her response clearly. The voice was in his head, but he could easily differentiate it from his own questioning thoughts. *But...you're a woman.*

"Male and female are distinctions we make in the physical world. Here, no such distinction exists."

Where are you?

"I'm everywhere that you are. I'm always with you. Your dreams are my dreams; your experiences are mine too. We're inseparable."

But you're not...real.

"We're the same, Gavin."

The conversation was going in a different direction than he'd anticipated, and suddenly Gavin felt himself getting frustrated. *What does that mean, that I'm not real either?* It was a question that had been pressing on his mind. *How can I not be real? Ryan says stuff like that too, but it makes no sense. I'm alive. I breathe. If I stop breathing, I die. How is that not real?*

"Remember what I said about the ocean of energy we're all a part of."

Yeah.

"Feel yourself immersed in that ocean, Gavin," Kate's soothing voice instructed. "Flowing freely, lovingly carried by the current, at one with the energy. That's who you really are. You have the ability to focus on something and experience it in what seems like a real way, but you never stop being who you are—part of that great ocean."

So I'm just focusing right now—that's all this is? You're telling me this "experience" of being in jail for the past seventeen years hasn't been real? Gavin sighed. *I'd like to believe that.*

"I'm here to help you do that, Gavin," Kate replied. "I love you and I know who you are. I'm here to help you remember."

I love you, too. Gavin couldn't deny it any longer; he was in love with Kathryn Harding, the woman, and with Kate, the apparition, the goddess of his dreams. It felt good to acknowledge what he'd been feeling, but the questions continued. He had so many, and Kate was there—listening, knowing, and willing to answer them all.

So I'm creating this experience? he persisted, needing to find clarity on the subject. *Why would I do that? If I get to choose what I focus on and create it, why wouldn't I create an easy, comfortable life? Why aren't I rich and successful, or at least living a normal life like everybody else?*

"You've already created those things—many times. And you will again. But this time, you had specific desires that only this experience could help you fulfill."

What desires?

"You knew you were free," she explained. "Conceptually, you understood freedom completely and thoroughly, but you wanted to experience it in a new way." Kate spoke with an authority that Gavin didn't think to question. "You knew who you were with a knowing that can't be shaken, but you wanted to taste that identity so fully that even being branded as a murderer and spending years behind bars wouldn't stop you from realizing it."

As Gavin listened to Kate's words, he marveled at them. They sounded so profound, so true. Suddenly everything in his life up to that point made sense. All his years in prison seemed a small price to pay for that knowing.

So now that I know this, what do I do? Start over? Learn something new?

"You're just beginning to understand, Gavin," Kate reminded him. "You've provided yourself with the contrast necessary to evoke powerful desires. Now the fun begins. Now you get to see them manifest. You get to focus on the outcome of each desire and feel the invigorating, insatiable joy that coming into alignment with it brings."

How do I do that?

"You created this experience by your focus on it. You told yourself a story, believed it was true, and began living it. Now to change your circumstances, you just start telling a different story."

Chapter 5

"So where did you learn this stuff you're always talking about?"

"I've always known it." Ryan looked up from his task and shot a faint smile Gavin's way. "Are you saying you believe me now?"

"I'm not sure," Gavin hesitated, not wanting to admit his change of heart. "Maybe...some of it."

"You know it's true," Ryan asserted. "Deep down you know you believe it. It just feels right."

The kid was right. It was more of a feeling than any kind of rational belief, and it *was* coming from a place deep within. Gavin was still curious, however. Kate had helped him understand his reasons for choosing to spend so many years of his life in prison. Now he wondered if Ryan was there for the same reason.

"So why are you here?" Gavin inquired.

"To help you remember."

Ryan's response baffled him. "You're here...because of me?"

"You'll understand soon enough," Ryan responded, not really answering his question. "Things are going to get interesting, but just remember: you're a powerful creator, and you're in control of what happens to you. This is where life starts to get really fun."

Ryan had pretty much just repeated what Kate had told him in his dream. Gavin looked at the boy in shock, anxiety rising within him. He had no idea how to respond.

What's going on? he asked, hoping for some higher wisdom to reveal itself. *Am I losing my mind? I have conversations with a woman in my head, and as if that's not enough to get me committed, now this kid tells me the same things. Am I going crazy? Is this place finally getting to me?* Gavin started to feel extremely uncomfortable. His pulse quickened, and he began to perspire.

"You're not crazy," Ryan replied, somehow reading his thoughts. "All this and so much more is possible. Believe me. You're getting out of here soon, and you wanted to know this to prepare you for what's ahead. It might seem a little confusing now, but if you remember these things you'll be okay."

What things? And how do you know when I'm getting out of here? Gavin tried to ask, but his throat wouldn't let the words pass.

The all-too-familiar panic that had been frequenting his dreams and tormenting his mind at night suddenly took over his body. Beads of sweat ran down his face, and his legs threatened to give out. His heart began to race as the room started to spin out of control. Soon people were yelling orders and moving all around him.

He couldn't recall what happened after that. He knew he must have blacked out, because he awoke in the prison infirmary with no memory of how long he'd been there or what time of day it was.

When the double doors swung open, Gavin saw Kate walking toward him, smiling. She was a welcome sight; he couldn't think of anyone he would rather see. Neither said a word for a moment. Then she reached out, gently touching his hand. "You're going to be all right, Gavin. The doctor said that you had a panic attack. Is this the first time you've experienced anything like this?"

"No." He was relieved to finally tell Kate about the things that had been happening to him. "I wake up feeling like that almost every night."

"How long has this been going on?" She looked concerned.

"A few weeks."

Kate frowned. "You've never mentioned anything about it in our sessions." She was stating a fact; her tone held no rebuke. "Do you feel comfortable talking about it now?"

"I wanted to mention it, but…"

"You don't need to explain, Gavin. Do you mind if I ask you a few questions?"

Gavin shook his head in response. He was eager now to share what had been troubling him.

41

"Do you remember your dreams?"

"I'm terrified and usually running from something. I know it has to do with the killing. I get that sickening feeling and often look down to see blood on my hands. But I don't know what it means."

"Dreams are manifestations. They're directly related to the thoughts we think, the emotions we feel every day," Kate explained. "But they can be confusing, especially if we try to sort out the specific details. What's important here, Gavin, is how they make you feel. Your dreams are representative of things going on in other areas of your life. Has anything changed for you in the past few weeks? Can you think of anything that might have triggered this?"

The dreams had started soon after Ryan came to Swenton, but they also coincided with Kate's rehabilitation program. And that, Gavin couldn't understand. He looked at her, desperately wanting to tell her what he was feeling but not knowing how. Instead, he frowned and shook his head. "I…" he shrugged helplessly. "I don't know."

"May I?" She took his hand and held it in both of hers. He nodded, liking the silken feel of her touch.

Closing her eyes, she gently rubbed the back of his hand. As he listened to her breathing, Gavin watched her chest rise and fall and was mesmerized by the beauty and rhythm of it. Without even thinking to question what she was doing or why, he felt himself drift effortlessly into his private world, Kate with him.

They were on a calm river, relaxing in a dinghy, letting the river carry them. The scenery along the water was breathtaking. Trees in vibrant shades of orange, burgundy, and yellow decorated gentle banks. Fences climbed the slopes, attaching themselves to picturesque farms with red barns and two story houses. The houses all had shutters on the windows, and verandas that stretched across their width. Children played on the hills and in shallow water near the edge of the river. They waved as Gavin and Kate drifted by.

"Mmm, this is nice." Kate leaned her head back, taking in the perfection of the moment.

Gavin smiled at her. She was beautiful, elegant even. Her arms were draped over the sides of the raft, and her long, graceful legs were stretched out comfortably. He was happy just to watch her.

She lifted her head and smiled lovingly at him. "You don't have to be afraid anymore, Gavin."

In that moment Gavin felt no fear and wondered what she was referring to.

"You know who you are now. You know why you're here. You don't have to be afraid."

What am I afraid of? Gavin stared at her blankly.

She leaned forward, and taking his hand she looked at him, peering deep into his soul.

Gavin gazed at the amber flecks in her eyes for a moment before he closed his own in a deliberate attempt to concentrate. He wanted to remember; he needed to know what was causing the anxiety.

The familiar emotion returned quickly in response to his focus, and the scenery around him began to transform. The sky darkened, and a giant wave washed over them, heaving their little dinghy into the air.

He felt himself being thrown about, but instead of grabbing the raft to keep from going over the side, he pulled Kate to him, wanting to keep her safe. A second wave lifted them and this time sent them flying through the air.

"It's not real, Gavin," Kate breathed. "You can change it with your thoughts."

Gavin was scared, but Kate's words reminded him that in their make-believe world, a change of focus could create a whole new setting. With Kate in his arms, he closed his eyes and imagined them lying on a beach beside a tranquil lake. When he opened his eyes they were lying together as if they had been there all along. Only, she was completely dry, and he was soaked to the skin.

As he lay back exhausted, Kate gently stroked his cheek. "Are you okay?"

What happened?

"You focused on your fear and created a manifestation of it," she said. "But you changed your focus. You're in control now. You don't have to be afraid."

Gavin felt the immense power of Kate's words and for the first time was able to look at his situation clearly. He wasn't sure where the revelation had come from, but in that moment he knew precisely what was causing his fears.

He opened his physical eyes to see Kate still standing by his bed. "I know what I'm afraid of," he told her eagerly. "I'm afraid of getting out of prison. I'm afraid of what people will think of me, afraid I won't fit in."

"It's natural to feel that way, Gavin," Kate soothed. "You've spent nearly half your life in this place. You've adapted to it. It's what you're most familiar with. Nearly everyone in your position experiences the same kind of fear or apprehension. But I'm here to help you. We can make that transition easier for you. You don't have to be afraid anymore." She reiterated the words she'd said to him in his vision.

Gavin looked at Kate questioningly. "I don't understand what's happening." He shook his head, longing to bridge the gap between his two worlds.

"What do you mean, Gavin?"

"You and me…the visions…I don't know what's real anymore."

Before she could respond, the doors to the infirmary burst open as several people rushed in, one of them a guard carrying someone. A man was placed on a gurney, and the commotion continued as orders were shouted and carried out. Gavin turned his head to see Ryan lying motionless just a few feet away. His face was blue, and efforts to revive him seemed futile.

He continued to watch until the guard ceased his efforts and with a solemn look to the others, shook his head. At that point Gavin turned to see Kate's reaction, but she was no longer by his bed. She wasn't in the group that surrounded Ryan, either. He had no idea why she'd left or where she would have gone.

As he dealt with the shock of the incident he'd just witnessed, Gavin recalled Ryan's words: "You'll understand soon enough."

Gavin closed his eyes and turned away. He didn't understand. He couldn't make any sense of the bizarre things that were happening, and the troubling possibility that he might be suffering from some kind of mental breakdown began to weigh on him.

In the midst of his confusion, however, one clear thought prevailed. *I need to hold on to the things I learned from Kate and from Ryan.* Gavin didn't know what prompted it, but the thought was vehement, settling itself in his mind with a decisive knowing, assuring him that if their words were true, everything else would make sense as well.

Part 2
~Kathryn~

This reality that you think is so stable and solid is not at all…it's changing constantly. It's changing and becoming and morphing to the degree that you allow it.

—ABRAHAM-HICKS

Chapter 6

Kathryn paced back and forth nervously as her colleague sat drumming her nails on the desktop.

"Don't worry," Adele tried to encourage her friend. "We'll get the approval. They've pretty much assured us we'll get it this time."

"I know; I can feel it," Kathryn replied. "It's just that we've been here so many times before."

The phone finally rang, and the two women looked at each other spellbound. "This is it." Kathryn tried to allay her jitters as she picked up the receiver.

"Thank you," she responded, feeling a rush of excitement as she heard the words she'd been waiting so long for. "Thank you, sir!"

"We got it!" Adele stood to her feet triumphantly. "Any restrictions?"

"No, they've agreed to the full three-year funding and immediate go-ahead."

"Which prison?"

"Swenton. They've already been approached and are willing to cooperate fully. We can start next week."

Kathryn sat down at her desk to let the news settle. For two years they had been pushing to get the green light for their prison rehabilitation program, not to mention all the years it took to develop, the criticism she and her co-workers had endured, and the tireless hours she'd spent writing and rewriting the proposal, only to have it shot down repeatedly.

She knew the struggle and hard work wasn't over; in truth it had just begun. The board wanted to see positive results early if the funding was to continue. She knew the critics would be watching closely, too. But she didn't want to dwell on that now. She wanted to savor the victory.

Adele had already informed the rest of the staff, and rounds of cheering had ensued. She re-entered Kathryn's office holding up a bottle of champagne. "This baby's been waiting a long time; do you want to do the honors?"

"I'd love to!"

GAVIN FELT WEAK as he walked to the dining hall. Four days in the infirmary had taken a toll, and he was eager to get his strength back.

It had been four days free of panic attacks and nightmares, and he was grateful for the reprieve. He couldn't wait to see Kate again and talk to her about what had happened, especially now that they'd discussed the reason for his fear. But he was a little anxious, given her quick disappearance. He couldn't help but wonder if she suspected that he had feelings for her.

He filled his tray and joined the other men at his usual table. Stubby welcomed him with a friendly slap on the back, and others made uncharacteristically polite remarks about his recovery. Their behavior surprised him. He had expected to be the subject of their jokes after rumors inevitably spread that he'd had a panic attack.

He was curious to know what their response had been to the news of Ryan's suicide. No doubt they were happy to hear it, but Gavin found himself distressed as he glanced at the table Ryan had once occupied. He wasn't heartless. He'd come to know the kid, worked with him, talked with him. Despite Ryan's strange manner, he'd gotten to Gavin somehow, and it seemed tragic and utterly pointless that his life was over.

He wasn't in the mood to hear the guys joke about it so decided not to bring it up. As he listened, however, all he heard was the usual gossip, dirty jokes, and speculation about which movie would be showing on the weekend. It seemed as if life was back to normal.

Unfortunately, normal was far from what Gavin was feeling. He didn't even know what the word meant anymore.

"GOD, WHERE DID YOU get that dress?" Adele gasped as Kathryn walked into the adjoining hotel room. "A paper bag would have been more flattering."

"Flattering is not the look we're going for," Kathryn retorted, noticing her colleague's black dress pants and sensible blouse, wishing she'd chosen something similar. "Most of those men haven't seen women in a long time. We don't want to send the wrong message."

"Sorry," Adele laughed. "But I've never seen you look this frumpy. You're not wearing makeup, and your hair—I hope it's not going to cut off the circulation to your head, with it pulled back so tight."

"Are you finished?"

Adele nodded, still smiling.

Kathryn had just spent the last half-hour stressing over what to wear, and now it was too late to change. Besides, her primary goal that morning was to be heard. She didn't want the men looking at her as anything other than a professional. She had a program to offer that could change their lives, and she wanted to be taken seriously, wanted to make a difference. As she thought about the morning ahead, she subconsciously twisted her rings.

"Kathryn...your wedding rings?" Adele looked at her questioningly.

Kathryn had reluctantly stopped wearing her wedding rings several months earlier. It had been almost four years since her husband passed away, and her friends and family wanted her to move on. In their opinion she'd grieved long enough and at forty-two was still an eligible woman. But dating was the furthest thing from Kathryn's mind. She'd poured herself into her work, and now all that hard work was finally paying off.

"It sends a message," she said simply.

"Yes," Adele replied. "It does."

Kathryn heard the tone in Adele's voice. She knew she was being judged again for her choice to refrain from taking part in the dating game. But for Kathryn, the choice had been easy to make. She'd loved and been loved in return by a wonderful man for nearly twenty years. A love that deep and that special, though it had ended abruptly, was something to be treasured and remembered.

A relationship with someone new would defile the memories she held dear. It would obscure them, maybe even cause them to fade away altogether. The very thought scared Kathryn, because time itself was starting to do those things despite her efforts to keep it from happening.

"Well, let's get this show on the road," she said abruptly, wanting to put a stop to thoughts and feelings that had come crashing in unbidden and unwelcome. "We're meeting with the warden for a short conference and then addressing the men in an assembly format," she added, knowing that Adele was as aware of the details of this important first morning as she was. "I'd like to get a look at the facility while we're there, too." They were joined then by the two men that would be completing their team for the project, and the four of them left for the prison.

Kathryn's excitement was coupled with nervousness. She was confident as a public speaker, but this was new territory for her. Her audience was typically made up of peers in the mental health profession or graduate students wanting to expand their knowledge, not men being held against their will—forced, or as the warden had put it, "strongly encouraged" to participate in the program. It gave a whole new meaning to the term *captive audience*. Nevertheless, she was ready. She'd been preparing for this moment for a long time. She not only knew the material backward and forward, she believed in it wholeheartedly. She truly believed that she would see lives changed for the better.

GAVIN HALF LISTENED as announcements were made after breakfast. But when the warden began talking about a rehabilitation program being initiated at Swenton, he had Gavin's full attention. Frowning, he looked around to see what the men's response was. All he saw was the usual look of disinterest in their faces as the warden talked about incentives and told the men that the program was to begin that morning with a lecture in the prison auditorium.

"What the hell?" Gavin said just loud enough for Stubby to overhear.

"Yeah," Stubby whispered back. "I don't know what they think they're gonna accomplish with that. It's just another waste of Joe Taxpayer's money."

"But we already have a rehab program."

"Since when?"

Gavin glanced over to see if Stubby was playing him, but his look was dead serious.

"The rehab program," Gavin repeated. "It's been running for weeks already."

"Shit, Gavin," Stubby frowned. "You've been in the infirmary for nearly three weeks. You must have been hallucinating or something; Bruno said you were in pretty rough shape."

"Three weeks?" Gavin shook his head. "I don't remember…"

The men were beginning to file out of the dining hall, and Stubby stood up to leave. Gavin followed numbly. What he was hearing made no sense; he was more confused than ever.

"You got that weird virus," Stubby explained. "They didn't tell you anything?"

Gavin shook his head.

"About half a dozen others did, too. They quarantined the whole place. Yesterday was the first day we could have visitors. Word is several people in the city died from it—mostly old people, though."

"I had a virus?"

"They're calling it some fancy name, but it's a virus, and apparently it spreads as easy as the common cold. Had the whole city in a panic for a while."

"And we don't already have a rehab program?"

Stubby frowned at him again, and Gavin started to think he'd better keep his inquiries to himself. There was just one more thing he needed to know. "The new kid…Ryan. Did he really do himself in?"

"Who?" Stubby shook his head. "I think you need to recuperate a few more days, buddy. We don't want rumors spreading. Keep this up," he laughed, "and the only day pass you'll be eligible for is to the psych ward at Dellberg."

WHILE KATHRYN and her associates waited in the wings, she listened to the men assemble. Talking and laughter filled the auditorium, chairs were being moved, and guards barked out commands. Once the men settled down, the warden nodded for her to begin. They had decided to forgo an introduction; she simply walked to the center of the platform where a small podium stood.

She'd been warned about the response she was likely to receive but was still surprised when the men responded with cheers, whistles, and even catcalls. It took a few moments before the guards got them settled down.

As she waited for silence, Kathryn looked over the group in front of her. The men differed in age, size, race, and most undoubtedly, belief systems. The one common denominator was that they were all serving time for committing a very serious crime, and that time was nearing an end.

One man in particular caught her attention. He was a large man, well built and handsome. The look he gave her was unmistakably different from ones the other men were directing at her. His expression was one of surprise and confusion, as if he knew her. As their eyes met and held for a moment, she wondered what his story was.

She anticipated learning about the men before meeting with them in the group and individual sessions. The warden had a package made up, a profile on each of the men for her and her associates to look over and keep in their files. It would assist greatly in tailoring the program to the individual needs of the men they would soon be working with.

Kathryn began by introducing herself and describing the program in general terms. The men were not taking her seriously, so she decided to get to the heart of her message, which was the essence of the teaching and what it would do for them. Having gained the men's attention, she made the most of it. She gave them a glimpse of the potentially life-changing program, and the processes and tools they could use to make their transition back into society. She assured them that the valuable teaching would help them in every area of their lives, both now and in the future.

As she spoke, she occasionally glanced at the man who had been and was still looking at her oddly. At one point, she saw him shake his head in what she could only describe as dismay. It was subtle; the others around him probably wouldn't notice. But her training caused her to pick up on behavior that was out of the ordinary, and his definitely stood out to her.

Kathryn ended her speech by describing how the program would be set up. She then introduced her colleagues. With that, she thanked the men for their willing participation and left them with the promise that they would not regret it.

The warden stepped forward to dismiss the men, and Kathryn watched as they filed out of the room. The man that had intrigued her was the last to get up from his chair, and as he left the room he turned to look directly at her. His face was clearly imprinted in her mind, and she was eager to go back to her hotel room and look through his profile.

In the meantime, she was elated to have made her presentation and to have seen the men and the facility first hand. It was all beginning to sink in. Her program, which for so long had been just an idea, a theory, was now unfolding into an undeniable reality. Kathryn couldn't have been more excited.

Chapter 7

Gavin wondered if he wasn't still in some sort of delusional state. The events of the past few weeks were unclear. He honestly couldn't remember what was real and what he had dreamed. He seriously considered reporting back to the infirmary to let them know he was hallucinating.

The most bizarre thing was that he had now sat through Kate's presentation—the same identical speech—twice. In fact, as he looked back on the first time he'd heard it, he realized that everything about that day mirrored the current one. She and her associates were wearing the same clothes, the men around him had uttered the same rude comments, and the guards had responded in the same way. Now, as they walked to the industry area, he heard Stubby make the same comment about rehabilitation that he'd made weeks earlier.

Gavin kept his thoughts to himself. He had a lot to sort out—if that were even a possibility. He had to try to make sense of it somehow. He knew he wasn't crazy. Unfortunately, he knew that no one else would see it that way.

KATHRYN AND HER TEAM had plenty to do in the days following her initial presentation. They were staying in a hotel but needed to find more permanent accommodation. If all went well, they would be located there for the full three years.

They also needed to go over the files and get familiar with the men that were to be part of the program. They would be dividing the men into four groups of nine or ten. She and her team members would remain with their respective groups for the duration of the program. Kathryn, being the project coordinator, would make the final decisions about placement of the men in each group, but she valued her associates input. They each had different strengths and abilities, and some of the men would be more suited to one than the other.

The profiles the warden had given them were detailed. Each included a picture, background information, details of the crime committed, and pertinent information about their stay in Swenton.

Adele walked into the room just as she finished reading Gavin McDermott's file. "This one interests me," Kathryn commented, glancing at her friend. "I was watching him while I made the presentation; he exhibited some odd behavior."

"What do you mean by odd?"

"His reaction was not in keeping with the response of the group as a whole," Kathryn explained. "At first he looked at me as if he knew me, as if he was surprised to see me or something. Then as the talk progressed he seemed distressed. I'd hoped to find something in his file that would explain it, but I'm baffled," she admitted.

"Yes," Adele replied. "I've looked at his file. He appears to be an exemplary prisoner, highly regarded by the other men and the prison staff. He's tried to better himself with education and training. There's no mention of unusual behavior."

"I'm going to put him in my group," Kathryn said decisively. "I'm curious. There's more to him than meets the eye. I'd like to find out what it is."

"I looked over the profiles and came up with a list of men I felt I'd be most suited to work with," Adele said, handing Kathryn a list.

"Great, thanks," Kathryn responded absently, still perusing the file that lay open in front of her. "He was in the infirmary recently," she remarked, turning over one of the pages. "It says here he and five other prisoners contracted the Srela virus. They quarantined the whole prison because of it. He must have been really sick; he was in the infirmary for three weeks. In fact, he was released the day we were there. That might explain some of what I observed."

"Possibly," Adele replied as she walked out.

Kathryn was so absorbed she didn't notice that Adele had gone back to her room. She continued reading the file and making notes, summing up what she'd learned about Gavin McDermott. He had been in Swenton for seventeen years, four months, and six days. He was eligible for parole within the year. He'd studied to get his high-school diploma and gone on to get his liberal arts degree. He'd worked his way up to become a supervisor in the prison's millwork shop. He had no infractions, no complaints from the guards or warden, current or previous. He exhibited leadership qualities, partook in sports, enjoyed woodworking, reading, and working out. He kept himself in good physical shape; Kathryn couldn't help but notice that detail when she was at the prison.

She tried to dismiss the image from her mind as she turned back to the pile of paperwork on the bed in front of her. She couldn't afford to put too much attention on one man. She needed to organize the groups that would be starting in just two days, and fax the information to the warden. As she looked over the lists of names her associates had given her, she was relieved to find that it was relatively easy to divide the men into four groups.

Everything was falling into place nicely. With lists ready to fax to the prison, Kathryn turned her attention to the ten men she had selected for her group. She'd included ones she felt would qualify to participate in her extended program. The program had not yet been approved. It depended on the success of the initial sessions. But Kathryn was confident, and she wanted to hand pick the small group of men that with her help would successfully re-establish themselves outside the prison walls.

SOME OF THE OLDER MEN shied away from learning, especially about computers, but technology didn't intimidate Gavin. He embraced it. He saw it as his connection with the outside world that he would soon be a part of again. He'd learned all he could, first from the volunteers that came to Swenton, then from courses offered online. He marveled at the Internet, the connection it gave him, the knowledge it held. He'd never hesitated to research any subject that interested him, and now he knew it held the answers he desperately wanted.

Gavin wasn't willing to entertain the possibility that he was crazy, nor was he willing to let anyone else brand him with that label. He was determined to find an explanation for what had happened to him, and the Internet was the place to look. He googled words and phrases. He even asked direct questions of the mighty cyber guru. Anything he felt might relate to his situation was directed to the source of all knowing, disguised as a humble, aged computer.

As he sat seeking direction in front of the monitor one evening, he summed up what he felt were the "facts" in the whole affair. Gavin was using the term loosely. He was also careful to keep his thoughts and speculations, and especially his findings, to himself. He refused to write anything down, even though keeping notes would have been beneficial to his cause.

I sat through Kate's introduction twice now. I know I did, he insisted. *The second time, I knew what she was going to say before she said it. And those sessions with her…the counseling felt real. The other times together… well, I know I imagined those.* He couldn't help thinking back to their exhilarating adventures and the times they'd kissed.

*And Ryan…*he continued. *I met him. I talked to him. I saw him die, and yet nobody else remembers him. It's like the kid never existed.*

Then there's the fact that I spent nearly three weeks in the infirmary, during which time I believed all this to be happening. He shook his head. It was too simple an explanation to dismiss it as hallucinations brought on by a high fever, especially now that Kate was real and was beginning her rehabilitation program—the same program he'd already taken part in.

What about all I learned? Gavin asked himself. *The meditation techniques and everything else Kate taught me, like my reason for being here. Where did all that come from? And what about the things Ryan said?* As strange as the kid was, Gavin couldn't argue with his words—many of which lined up with Kate's teaching.

Gavin had been trying to escape in his mind, but Kate's guided meditations had taken him to a whole new level. They'd left him intoxicated, wanting more.

He'd learned to create with his thoughts and even change the outcome of his creations with a change of focus. Not only that but he'd fallen in love.

I saw the future, for God's sake! He felt himself getting frustrated. *I met Kate, somehow, before she even came here. That must mean something!*

Back to his task, he googled "premonition," "out-of-body experience," and "paranormal." Premonition was being defined as a forewarning, intuition, hunch, or feeling. *No,* Gavin decided, *it was more than a feeling. I experienced it.*

Literally hundreds of thousands of sites came up under the other terms he'd typed, and for a moment he felt overwhelmed at the prospect of having to wade through so much information. Then he remembered something Kate had said to him: "Reality is a tricky thing." Ryan had said much the same: "None of this is real, you know."

That was the direction Gavin needed. He had to learn all he could about reality—what it was, what it wasn't, what other people had to say about it. He typed in the word and sat back with a sense of anticipation, knowing that the answer to his deepest questions could be a mouse click away.

KATHRYN AND HER ASSOCIATES arrived early for the first day of group sessions. She was tingling with excitement and a little nervousness as she prepared the room for her group. She set ten chairs in a semicircle, leaving a space for herself and an easel she'd brought along. On the whiteboard surface, she wrote the famous lines from Shakespeare's *As You Like It*: "All the world's a stage and all the men and women merely players. They have their exits and their entrances, and one man in his time plays many parts."

She chose the quotation to emphasize specific truths she wanted to convey. The first was that all men and women were essentially the same, and the second—the one she intended to stress repeatedly throughout the program—was that the men were more than what they saw in themselves. What they were experiencing was merely an act, a scene from the play called life. It didn't need to define who they were or what they chose to experience as they moved on with their lives.

The program had received much criticism from its opponents. The basis of the teaching was that a person created his or her own reality through thought, whether consciously or not. It was an age-old teaching that had surfaced briefly and sporadically throughout the centuries. In recent years the idea had caught on suddenly and become a worldwide phenomenon. The nations' talk show hosts heralded it, making "Law of Attraction" a household term. But as fads do, it eventually subsided to be replaced by the next latest craze.

Its overnight stardom, however, had caused it to become the subject of debate at one of the most prestigious universities in the nation. Out of that debate was born the determination to prove the theory's validity. After many years it was finally being acknowledged and was now the foundational teaching of the trial program that was about to begin. Kathryn was thrilled and honored to be part of it, not just because it was history in the making, but because the men at Swenton had so much to gain by receiving it.

Her late husband had done most of the research; he'd made tremendous breakthroughs in the world of psychology and modern medicine with his findings. Kathryn was immensely proud of the work he'd done, glad too that he'd been recognized with the Nobel Prize before his untimely death.

She had picked up where her husband left off, and now Kathryn was charting new territory. Backed by years of research, acknowledged by professionals in various fields, and supported with government funding, she was nevertheless heading into the unknown, the untried. Along with the excitement, she felt a slight burden of responsibility, as if the success of the program was now up to her. The fulfillment of her husband's hopes and dreams, his life's greatest work, was on her shoulders.

The thoughts lowered her vibration, so she quickly banished them. They weren't in keeping with what she believed or what she planned to impart to the men in just a few moments. She truly believed that success wasn't simply about the accomplishments or the awards. Success could best be measured by the amount of joy in a person's life.

As she heard the door open, she looked up and smiled; her students had arrived; her program had begun.

Chapter 8

As he entered the room, Gavin noticed the difference right away. Kate was wearing a different outfit than she had for the 'first' first session he had attended. As well, he noticed the words written on the white board. Neither the easel nor the quotation had been part of the session Gavin had already attended.

As he listened, he noted more differences. She introduced herself as Kathryn, not Kate. She seemed more formal, somehow, than the woman he'd come to know.

He filed his observations with the rest of the data he'd collected in the past few days. He still didn't have clear answers, but he was getting closer; he could feel it. It was a treasure hunt of sorts. Each clue led to another. He'd found several interesting websites and had come across the name of a book that he was able to have transferred from the city library. He was devouring it in his cell at night.

Reality was a topic of which everyone from Albert Einstein to Shirley MacLaine had something to say. He was happy to find that science wasn't silent on the subject. He had read about a man named Heisenburg, the cofounder of quantum physics, who taught that atoms were not things but rather tendencies. Another man claimed that everything people see and experience is essentially nothing more than a hologram. It was a fascinating subject—one Gavin had barely begun to touch on.

Watching Kate closely as she led the session, Gavin noted that certain elements mirrored the first. The guided meditation was nearly the same and the theme of her message unchanged. Gavin silently questioned the differences. *If I was foreseeing the future, then why is this future different from the one I observed? What would cause it to be altered in these seemingly insignificant ways?*

He saw Kate look at him once or twice during the session. At one point, as he caught her eye, he sent her a silent message. It seemed foolish and maybe even futile, but he had to try. The thing was, he wasn't sure if it was the woman before him he was directing it to or rather some unconscious inner part of her that he had connected with, a part that he longed to connect with again.

AS THE DAYS PROGRESSED, Kathryn was satisfied with the progress of her group sessions. She'd received positive assessments from her colleagues as well. That was good because in a week she was meeting with the board of directors of the university, along with government officials, to give them a report.

Individual sessions were about to start, and Kathryn was eager to begin the one-on-one time. This was where real accomplishments would take place because she could tailor her teaching to the men's individual needs and move forward at the pace their level of understanding allowed.

Some of her students were having a hard time with the new ideas, whereas others seemed to grasp them easily. A couple of the men, however, were difficult to read, and Gavin McDermott was one of them. He watched her constantly; she knew he was paying attention. She could tell he was enjoying the meditations, but he was quiet, answering an occasional question but never speaking unless spoken to. She still felt there was more to him than what she was observing, and she hoped to uncover it in their time together that morning.

Gavin arrived promptly at the scheduled time, and Kathryn smiled to welcome him. He seemed uncomfortable—more so than usual—so she tried to engage him in casual conversation before they began. She asked how he'd been enjoying the group sessions.

"Fine."

"Do you have any questions or concerns about the program?"

"No, not really," he shrugged.

Getting information out of him was like pulling teeth, but she persevered, wanting to help him relax and get past the awkwardness he seemed to be feeling.

"Gavin, how do you feel, overall, about your prison term?" she ventured. "Especially now that you're nearing your release date?"

She watched him take a deep breath and saw what appeared to be relief on his face. He looked her in the eye and held her gaze.

"I realized I'm kind of scared of what it'll be like on the outside." He exhaled, now visibly relieved, as if sharing his feelings had been extremely difficult yet rewarding at the same time.

She smiled and touched his arm in a comforting gesture—something she knew was wrong, but she'd not stopped to think. She was grateful that he felt free to share something so personal. "Gavin, that's perfectly normal. I'm going to help you through that. I'm going to give you the tools you need to make the transition as painless as possible."

KATE'S WORDS ECHOED ones she'd used to comfort him in the infirmary after helping him discover what was causing his panic attacks. Hearing them, Gavin longed to connect with her as he had in the past, but he had no idea how to do it or if it was even possible.

"Thanks," he replied. "I like what you've been teaching us so far. It makes sense."

"How would you describe yourself, Gavin?"

Gavin recognized the question and knew the direction Kate was going. Suddenly he wondered something. *Can I change what happens here today? Because I already know the outcome, can I change or influence it? Is that why some of the sessions have been slightly different? Because of what I know?*

It made sense; it explained why events were unfolding as they were. Having seen the future, he could now influence and maybe alter what was about to happen.

Still apprehensive but compelled to prove his theory, he decided to ask a question that would take their session in a different direction. "Kate, I was wondering..." he began tentatively. "I've heard you say that we create our own reality. What is reality anyway?"

KATHRYN STARED AT GAVIN for a moment. Dumbfounded, she opened her mouth to speak but had to close it again when nothing came out. She'd been thrown some intense questions before by scientists, fellow psychologists, and others determined to find a flaw in the theory. But this was different; Gavin had asked a question that some of the greatest thinkers in her field couldn't answer. As unexpected as the question was, however, it was the casual way he'd called her Kate that really unnerved her.

Before her husband died, he'd been asking that question. None of the existing explanations satisfied him, and he'd become obsessed, not just with finding an answer but with proving it scientifically. Moreover, he was the only other person to call her Kate since she'd become an adult.

Kathryn knew she had to respond, and she had to remain professional. She quickly collected herself and smiled. "I'm sorry, Gavin. Your question caught me off guard. We can talk about that if you like."

She was about to mention that she preferred to be called Kathryn, but she hesitated. She didn't want to offend Gavin. He knew nothing of her past and was simply being less formal with her as he loosened up. That was something she wanted to encourage. She decided to let it pass.

"Teachers are varied on the subject of reality," she explained. "Its definition ranges from the literal here and now to a temporal, fleeting experience that exists only in our minds."

"What do you believe?"

Kathryn knew she was being tested. She had some ideas about reality. She certainly believed that a person's thoughts influenced the outcome of their experience, thus creating their reality, but she hadn't come to any definite conclusions about the specific nature of reality itself, although she'd questioned it often. She searched her mind for a sufficient answer but found none.

"In science, we're trained to look at things as they are—black and white. But I've seen plenty of grey that can't be overlooked, or easily explained for that matter. My..." She decided against mentioning her husband. "Great men and women have proved there's more to 'what is' than just what is."

He continued to watch her silently, and she realized she'd sidestepped his question.

"I believe we can influence, even change our reality," she offered, knowing it wasn't what he was looking for. "I believe the mind is powerful and capable of much, much more than we've previously believed possible."

Kathryn smiled and shook her head, admitting defeat. "Gavin, I'm sorry; I can't give you a proper definition of the word; it's something I'm still trying to settle in my own mind. I do think, however, the fact that great minds can't agree on a definition does reveal something about the true nature of the subject."

GAVIN APPRECIATED Kate's honesty. He also saw that his question made her uncomfortable. He hadn't meant to do that, and he regretted asking. He had proved his theory correct, however. He'd changed the direction of the discussion by asking a question that hadn't been part of the original session. Satisfied, he gave the reins back to Kate. "Sorry, I didn't mean to get you sidetracked. You probably have a plan that you follow. I hope I didn't mess that up."

"No, of course not," she replied graciously. "These sessions are just a trial, really. I'm learning, too. I'll probably make significant changes to the program once I evaluate the outcome here. So please feel free to ask any questions you like."

"You asked how I'd describe myself," he offered, gazing at the familiar shape of her face and noticing the unusual blend of hazel and green in her eyes. "I know I'm more than just a prisoner here. I'm a son, a brother, a friend…I'm a supervisor in the prison's millwork shop, too."

Gavin had a distinct advantage over Kate—knowing what she was going to ask and knowing how to answer her questions—and he felt guilty when he saw that it put her in a less than confident position as his teacher and guide.

"That's very insightful, Gavin," she responded genially. "There's much more to you than your experience at Swenton. You're part of something bigger. We all are. We're vibrational beings living in a vibrational universe. We're equipped with a highly sensitive guidance system that, once we learn to follow, leads us to be and do and have all that we've come here to experience."

"How do we know what we've come here to experience?" Gavin asked. Kate had answered the question for him in his dreams, but he longed to talk more about the subject.

"We all have desires, Gavin, and those desires call us forward. Our emotions offer us a moment by moment guidance system, telling us whether or not we're in alignment with our desires. When we feel good and follow the inspired action that flows out of the positive emotion, we're going in the right direction. If we continue in that direction we'll see the fulfillment of all that we've asked for.

"However, most of us feel bad consistently enough that we become immune to our guidance, and then we wonder why life never turns out for us like it does for those lucky few that are living their dreams."

Kate's words, although practical, lacked the depth and insight of the wisdom she'd previously shared with him. He was beginning to wonder if he'd connected with a part of her that she wasn't fully aware of yet.

"But can we know what our life's purpose is?" Gavin continued pursuing the topic. He understood why his past had unfolded the way it had; it was a manifestation of his thoughts and desires, some of which he'd set into motion before he began this physical experience. But now the future that loomed before him was a blank slate, and he wanted to know what it held for him or what he was to do with it. "...beyond this moment, I mean. Is it possible to get a glimpse of our future?"

Chapter 9

Kathryn didn't know what to make of Gavin Mc-Dermott. She had rightly sensed that there was more to him than was evident at first glance. His questions amazed and baffled her. His level of intelligence and deep, analytical mind impressed her, as did his gentle personality. It was hard to imagine that he'd ever harmed anyone, let alone taken a life. He was obviously a different person than he had been seventeen years earlier.

He was the perfect student, really: open and hungry to learn but knowledgeable enough to contribute to the conversation. He challenged her to dig deeper and learn more. She never knew what he was going to come up with, and more than once she'd had to allay him with the promise that she would get back to him with the answer to his question. Nevertheless, she thoroughly enjoyed their sessions together.

She was discussing him one evening with Adele in the apartment they shared. "It's a little unnerving sometimes," she admitted. "I'm supposed to know all the answers, but I don't. He really keeps me on my toes."

"Where do you think he's gotten his information?" Adele asked and then answered her own question. "The Internet, maybe, or books. But from what you've said, it seems like he's tapped into some higher knowing, too. He seems really connected. What's his spiritual background?"

"He *is* very connected," Kathryn replied. "I think that's what I sensed about him from the start. He was raised catholic; his parents attend church regularly. We've talked a little about his beliefs. He definitely believes in a higher power but doesn't hold rigidly to the Catholic teachings. It's the way he looks at me, though…" Kathryn added.

"What do you mean?"

"I don't know for sure. It's like…" she stopped, not sure how to describe the way he made her feel. "It's almost like he knows me. The questions he asks, the comments he makes—I'd swear sometimes he's peeked at my notes. He'll answer questions that I'm just about to ask."

"That *is* strange."

"There's something else."

Adele turned from the skirt she was pressing, giving Kathryn her attention. "That sounds serious. What is it?"

"He calls me Kate," she replied, "even though I introduced myself as Kathryn. He didn't talk much at first. I thought he was shy or maybe a little uncomfortable with the one-on-one format, but now I think he was just reading me."

"But why...? Oh shit!" Adele pulled the iron away from the fabric too late. "I scorched it." She began to laugh. "You know, every time I wear this skirt, I'm reminded how much I dislike it. I think, subconsciously, I was looking for a way to ruin it. I'm going to have to start paying closer attention to my guidance system," she declared, tossing the garment aside.

"So why do you think Gavin calls you Kate and not Kathryn?" she asked, now fully focused on the conversation.

"I don't know," Kathryn shrugged. "I was tempted to correct him the first time, but I wanted him to feel comfortable with me so I let it go. It's been several weeks now. I can't very well tell him he's been wrong this whole time."

"Is he wrong?"

Kathryn recognized Adele's tone. She knew what her friend was getting at, too. She had been christened Patricia Katherine, after her two grandmothers. She was called Kate for short, which wasn't a bad name, just a little too easy to rhyme when the other kids teased a shy, chubby little girl. Her father liked to call her Patty-Kate, a name that might have been endearing had he not been intoxicated for most of her formative years.

It wasn't until after her twenty-first birthday that anyone called her by a different name. At that juncture in her life, she decided to make some changes. Having been raised in a dysfunctional home, she was determined to create a life for herself that was radically different from the one she'd known. A brand new career, a new city, and a new more sophisticated name—they all represented a clean start in life.

A year later when she met a wonderful man and fell in love for the first time, he called her Kate while making love to her, and she couldn't bear to correct him. Kate became his choice name for her, and she didn't mind it. But now hearing it from Gavin left her with all kinds of confusing emotions.

"You know, I think there's a Kate inside you, and she's trying to get out," Adele said frankly.

"Why do you say that?"

"Think about it; the name Kate sounds young and fun loving, adventurous and carefree. I think you are those things deep down inside, and I think you need to let that part of you out once in a while. Kathryn has a certain elegance and sophistication to it, but it also feels somewhat cold and unapproachable, contrived somehow, like you're pretending to be something you're not."

The candid remarks stunned Kathryn. Adele was straightforward when it came to her opinions, and Kathryn wasn't usually offended by the things she said. This time Adele's words hit a tender spot, and Kathryn realized she had some work to do.

Adele quickly responded to Kathryn's silence with an apology as she touched her arm lovingly. "I didn't mean that as an insult, sweetie. I know you've been through your share of rough times. But you deserve to feel good. Maybe it's time to admit that it's okay to feel good again."

Kathryn looked at Adele with tears swelling in her eyes, but no words would come. Her friend was right; she could feel it.

"Kathryn, maybe Gavin *can* read you. Maybe he calls you Kate because he can see that hidden part of you. The Universe uses all kinds of people in our lives to teach us and remind us. No labels, remember. He's your teacher as much as you're his."

"You're right," Kathryn said, blinking back tears. "You're absolutely right."

GAVIN WAS GLAD to have someone unbiased to talk to about what he was experiencing. He'd found that person on a social networking site, and "Retro57" was now his cybernet friend.

He'd come across the site as he browsed the Internet, looking for information. Interacting that way was new for Gavin, yet fun in a strange, delusional kind of way. He'd created a persona with a name, a job, a belief system, even a love interest. It was nice to feel like an ordinary person, talking about ordinary things with another guy. They talked about extraordinary things too. Retro had some deep questions, and he liked to hear what Gavin, or "Free2B," as he called himself online, had to say.

His friend had some great advice. He was supportive of Gavin's ideas and encouraging when Gavin felt down. Because of their shared interest in the paranormal, many of their conversations dealt with that subject. They both loved reading and often posted what they were learning.

"Hey F2B," Retro typed. "Just finished a book by a guy named Scheinfeld. I think you'd like it. It's mind blowing. Get this: 'Everything you perceive with your five senses is an illusion—all props and special effects designed to create an alternative reality that allows you to play the human game.' Shit, man, what if that's true? What if it's all an illusion? I'll send you a link to his website₁. Check it out."

"I know those kinds of ideas seem far fetched," Gavin replied, "but I'm starting to believe they're true. Thanks for the link; I'll pick up a copy of the book." He made a mental note to request the book from the library. "The part about our five senses being an illusion, that's interesting. Deepak Chopra says it a little differently: 'Only the present, which is our awareness, is real and eternal.' He describes everything else as a field of possibilities. He says that in our willingness to step into that field, we surrender ourselves to the creative mind that orchestrates the dance of the universe."

"So what's real then?" Retro asked.

"I'm beginning to think that 'real' is whatever we want to define it as," Gavin replied. "Personally, I like the idea of calling something real. If you think about it, it's our awareness of something that makes it seem real. But like Deepak says, that only exists in the present moment. The past doesn't exist at all, except in our memory, and the future…well, that's a little complicated.

"There's power in the moment that doesn't exist anywhere else," he continued. "So the present moment is real in that sense. We just have to stop limiting the term *real* to only the tangible and the concrete."

"Good point," Retro responded. "But what do you mean about the future being complicated?"

"Something happened to me. It's kind of out there," Gavin admitted. "I had an experience that felt totally real. I was interacting with people, having conversations, feeling things. Let's just say all my senses were involved. I'm not sure if it was a dream or an out-of-body experience or if I stepped into some sort of alternate reality, but I woke up to find that none of it had really happened.

"Right after that, some of the things I dreamed about started happening. I experienced one full day that felt like the movie *Groundhog Day*. I knew what was going to happen and what people were going to say. Then things started to alter slightly. Each day after that was more removed from the original version.

"What I noticed right away was that when something familiar happened, I could react the way I had in my dream and predict the outcome, or I could deviate from the dream, change the variables, and the outcome would be totally different. It didn't take long—a couple of weeks—till I'd altered things enough that nothing was predictable anymore."

"Holy shit! No wonder you're so messed up!" Retro exclaimed. "Just kidding, buddy. That's out there all right. I envy you, though; I'd love to experience those kinds of things."

Gavin felt relieved to admit some of the strange occurrences to another person, albeit this person might be a figment of his imagination, too. Whoever he was, real or imagined, it felt good to have a friend.

Gavin headed back to his cell. He enjoyed his time on the computer, but it was severely limited. His whole life was severely limited for that matter. Yet what he was learning told him that none of the limitation was real, that it was just an experience he'd created.

'Reality' was definitely an illusive concept. It could be nothing or it could be everything; it could be whatever a person assigned it to be.

Having read Don Miguel Ruiz's books, Gavin resonated with the author's analogy of a movie theater. It helped him make some sense of the term. Reality was like his own personal movie theatre. In any given moment, the things that were happening were like a movie showing on a giant screen, and he was the observer. However, his movie was just one of many that were playing around him. Others were sitting in their own theater, viewing their own version of life, and it was possible to get tripped up if he tried to see what other people were watching. Gavin believed that his focus determined which movie he watched, and even more important, his thoughts dictated the outcome of the movie itself.

He liked the analogy because Kate had taught him that he had control over what he chose to think about. And the idea of a private movie theatre was similar to the personal space Kate had the men create in their guided meditations.

He smiled as Kate came to mind. She did often, now, and he welcomed her into his thoughts. She had yet to do a guided meditation in their individual sessions. Gavin was tempted to suggest it, but he so enjoyed their conversations and sensed that she did as well.

Besides, he'd practiced the meditations in his cell at night until he could imagine Kate's voice guiding him and joining him in his adventures. He talked to her, too. He asked her questions and received answers. And more often than not, the information he received was the topic of conversation in their next session.

He truly wished that he could talk to the physical Kate and explain what was going on between them, or at least try to explain it. He felt he owed her that. He wondered if at any level she felt the connection between them, if she experienced any of the things he did but was unable, because of their situations, to admit it.

Chapter 10

Kathryn was excited to share the news with Gavin. Because of her recommendation to the parole board, he had been granted an escorted day pass. It was a full three months before his name was supposed to come up before the board, and in many cases, inmates were denied the first time without their files being looked at.

She'd submitted a recommendation for another man too, but his application had been turned down without explanation. Kathryn suspected it was a test, a way for them to evaluate the work she was doing. In any case, she was glad it had been Gavin and not the other man they had chosen. Gavin's progress was more substantial, and she believed his transition would go the smoothest.

She'd already spoken with Gavin's parents, telling them the news and making plans for the first outing, which would be a trip home to spend the day with them. Now it was her responsibility as well as her honor to tell Gavin. She couldn't hide her enthusiasm when Gavin arrived for his session, and he gave her a questioning look as he sat down.

"I have good news," she said.

"They're letting me out?" Gavin asked somewhat sarcastically, yet Kathryn sensed he knew.

"Um…yes," she frowned and then laughed. "Yes! You've been approved for a day pass!"

Gavin didn't respond, and Kathryn couldn't read him. His face was expressionless, his eyes focused on the floor.

"Gavin, are you okay?"

He spoke without looking up. "I had a dream last night," he said softly. "I was sitting in my parents' living room. You were there."

Before she could respond, he added, "I thought it was just…I mean, I like to imagine sometimes…it helps me get through the night."

"It's real, Gavin," Kathryn assured him. "It's set for Thursday. You have a twelve-hour pass. Your parents know; I've already spoken to them. I'll be escorting you home."

He looked at her, and she saw a slight smile flash across his face, but there was something else. "Did I create this?"

"Yes, Gavin, you did."

"What did my parents say?"

"Your mom was crying. She couldn't speak at first. Your dad picked up the other line, and I gave them the details. They were excited and thanked me…several times. Oh yeah," she remembered, "your dad asked me to tell you that he finally got the TV hooked up."

"My sister bought Dad a 42 inch plasma TV for his birthday last month and got him set up with a satellite dish. They still had the set I used to watch eighteen years ago. Dad likes sports, but he'd often listen to games on the radio because the old television had such poor reception." Gavin smiled and shook his head. "They're old school."

"They seem wonderful," Kathryn contended. "I'm looking forward to meeting them."

"Yeah," Gavin agreed. "They're pretty awesome."

"Gavin, in our first session, you mentioned that you felt scared at the thought of being on the outside. Do you still have those feelings?"

"I thought I was doing okay with that," he admitted. "But Kate...now that it's actually going to happen...I'm terrified."

Kathryn still felt strange when Gavin called her Kate, but she tried to ignore it. "Well, then," she suggested, "let's deal with that today. I'm going to make extra time to see you tomorrow too.

"Remember," she counseled. "Fear is just an emotion; it can't control you unless you let it. You get to decide what you want to think about."

"I'm going home; I ought to feel good."

"It doesn't work that way, Gavin," she explained. "Your mind may tell you that you should feel a certain way, but your emotions are always accurate, and there's benefit in listening to them. Let's talk about the fear. Can you feel the power in it?"

"Yeah, definitely…but it doesn't feel good."

"Let's not label it good or bad. For now, just feel the power of the emotion itself. I want you to close your eyes for a moment."

GAVIN CLOSED HIS EYES and listened to the sound of Kate's voice. He loved hearing it and normally it soothed him, but in that moment all he could think about was the dream he'd had the night before. He had been sitting in his parents' living room, just as he'd told Kate, and she was there with him. What he didn't mention, however, was that he had handcuffs on his wrists and shackles on his feet. He was home, yet he was still a prisoner.

"Tell me about your dream, Gavin," Kate urged, reading his thoughts.

He told her the details, and her response surprised him. "Gavin, imagine yourself sitting in your parents' living room, shackled and handcuffed, just like you were in the dream. I want you to remember what that felt like."

Gavin couldn't do otherwise.

"Now look down. Instead of cold, hard steel, fear is binding your hands and feet. Long strands of thickly woven emotion are holding you there, keeping you from moving."

Gavin did as Kate asked. In his mind, he looked down and saw what had him bound. Fear was wrapped tightly around his hands and his feet, just as she had described.

"It's your fear that is keeping you in prison, Gavin, even when you're sitting on the sofa in your parents' living room."

He nodded, realizing the truth of her statement.

"Remember what I said about fear," Kate continued. "It's just an emotion; it only has the power that you give it. I want you to imagine the fear dissolving. Shake your wrists; nothing's holding them now. Move your feet; they're free of the shackles."

Gavin began to move his hands and feet. He shook his wrists and shifted his feet back and forth. It felt good to be free of any restraints.

"Now I want you to think of the tremendous power that fear possessed, the power to hold you captive. Imagine taking it back, reclaiming what's yours. Imagine it flowing to you. Feel the power entering your body and filling you like a balloon with each deep, cleansing breath."

Gavin breathed deeply, wanting to reclaim all the power he could. He felt something wash over him like a wave, the reverberation spreading through his entire body. It was a rush like nothing he'd ever experienced before, and it left him tingling.

"You are the power, Gavin. Nothing else can claim that power unless you give it permission. It's you, Gavin. The power is you."

Kate stopped talking, and Gavin remained still for a minute, feeling the stimulating effects of the transfer of power$_2$. Then he looked at Kate and smiled, "That was really cool."

"How do you feel now?"

"I don't feel the fear anymore; it's like it's really gone. It was amazing to take back the power like that. But I still feel a little…" he hesitated.

"It's okay, Gavin, there's no right or wrong. The important thing here is to recognize how the emotions feel, then deal with them, not judge them."

"I feel kind of…pissed off." Gavin couldn't think of any other way to express how he was feeling at that moment.

"Okay, let's deal with that now. Does it feel like anger, or frustration? When you feel it, can you pinpoint any specific thoughts?"

"Yeah, it ticks me off that fear could have that much control over me. I think I'm angry at the fear." He shrugged and looked at Kate. "That probably doesn't make much sense."

"It does make sense, Gavin. Anger is a natural progression from fear. It makes perfect sense to be angry at something that had such a strong hold over you. Anger is actually more powerful than fear," Kathryn added. "Do you know why that is?"

Gavin shook his head.

"It's because you can channel it. You have more direct control over it. Anger is a very useful tool when you learn how to use it."

"Really?"

"It's true. Most people don't understand that and instead use it in a destructive or harmful way. That's why there's so much violence in the world. So many people live in fear and despair, which are extremely powerless emotions. They naturally reach for anger to take back their power, and it plays out in violent crimes, terrorism, and oppression. All countries that are at war are fighting for that very reason."

"Wow, I've never thought about it like that." Gavin was quiet for a moment. As he reflected on his own situation, he had to ask, "Do you think the crime I committed was because of that?"

"Do you feel ready to talk about it?"

"I'm not sure. I mean…I think I'd like to talk about it. I think it would help. But it doesn't feel like the right time."

AS SHE LISTENED to Gavin make a choice based on how he felt, Kathryn marveled again at the understanding he possessed. He was making tremendous progress in using his emotional guidance system to feel his way.

She smiled. "That's perfectly fine, Gavin. You'll know when the time is right. We were talking about the anger that you felt just now. Would you like to continue dealing with that?"

"Yeah, I would."

She led Gavin through another process of reclaiming his power, helping him find relief as he moved up the emotional scale. When their session ended, she could tell that he was feeling more positive about his upcoming trip home.

Kathryn looked forward to Thursday as well. She had some preparation to do before the day arrived, and she worked on it that evening at her apartment.

"What are you working on?" Adele asked.

"I have to submit an itinerary for Thursday."

"Seriously? You're driving him to his parents' farm. What more do they need to know?"

"We're not even supposed to make an unscheduled restroom stop," Kathryn laughed. "So I have to anticipate everything ahead of time and lay it all out for them—what route we'll take and where we plan to stop—that kind of thing."

"It'll be interesting to see the freedom we take for granted through the eyes of someone who's been incarcerated for so long," Adele remarked.

"I know," Kathryn said. "Gavin's kept up with a lot of the changes that have taken place since 1992, but he only knows *about* them. Now he gets to experience them firsthand. He's never watched a flat screen television, played a game on an Xbox, sent a text message, or owned a cell phone for that matter. He's never seen a GPS system in a vehicle. He's probably never even had a latte at Starbucks.

"This city has nearly doubled in size since he's seen it. His farm will probably look different than it did seventeen years ago. I'm trying to imagine what it's going to be like for him."

"It sounds exciting," Adele responded. "I can't wait to hear about it."

Kathryn finished the outline for the itinerary. She hoped the plans she'd made would be interesting without being too overwhelming for Gavin. There would be more outings to come—every two weeks if all went well.

She would be accompanying him and documenting his progress, submitting detailed reports to the prison board. He would be the first of the small experimental group that she'd be working closely with both within the prison walls and once they were released. She had two other men with parole hearings imminent, so her schedule would be full.

She had to admit, as unprofessional as it sounded, that she enjoyed her interaction with Gavin more than with the other men. He had unique qualities that continued to surprise and intrigue her. Absorbing the concepts easily, he was already applying the teaching in his life and continually asking questions that challenged her. He was a paradox in many ways: a boy in a grown man's body, a naïve young man with a wise old soul, a gentle giant incarcerated for murder.

Kathryn smiled. She couldn't deny that she was fond of him, but she understood the danger of getting emotionally attached to her students. Even more so, the danger of them becoming attached to her.

She didn't think it would be an issue with Gavin, however. Transference was a common problem in counselor-patient relationships, but Gavin was wise; he was also in tune with his emotions. She was quite sure his feelings for her didn't go beyond appreciation for the understanding he was gaining from her. At most, it extended to genuine friendship. And she didn't mind that; she would be honored to have him call her his friend.

Chapter 11

Gavin lay awake all night thinking about the approaching day. Anxious anticipation had replaced debilitating fear. It was a definite improvement, yet he found it annoying. What he really wanted to do was fall asleep and wake up just in time to leave. It was the waiting that was painful.

Kate had gone over the itinerary with him. He could see the entire day mapped out in his mind, yet it felt like he was stepping into a big black hole. It wasn't what was out there that was intimidating; it was simply the idea of being out after having been locked away for so long.

He tried a familiar meditation to calm himself, but the tranquil lake scene and Kate's soothing voice echoing softly in his head didn't have the same effect it had in the past, so he pictured his farm instead. As he visited the buildings and places he knew so well, Gavin began to relax and enjoy the tour. He saw himself taking Kate's hand and sharing the experience with her. Suddenly he was eager to spend the day together, driving with her, introducing her to his family, and showing her places he'd loved as a child.

He no longer questioned his feelings for Kate or for Kathryn. The two were the same, yet different. He didn't know where Kathryn ended and Kate began. One was an imaginary lover, the other his counselor. He wasn't willing to see it as crazy. He'd created it and Kate was a part of it. He couldn't explain it, but neither could he deny it. It just was.

Morning finally came, and Gavin went straight to the warden's office to receive his pass. Kate was already waiting with jacket on and keys in hand.

"Ready to go?"

"Oh yeah," he laughed. "Since about 2 a.m."

"Well, then," Kathryn grinned as she led the way toward the security doors. "You'll really appreciate the triple grandé cinnamon dolce americano misto I'm going to buy you."

"Is that coffee?"

"Like you've never had it before, my friend."

Kate seemed to be in an upbeat, playful mood, and Gavin liked what he heard and saw. She was dressed in jeans and a sweater, still somewhat conservative but definitely more casual than he'd ever seen her before.

He'd been imagining every detail and wanted to savor the feelings each step produced. As they walked past the guards at the main entrance, one smiled as he acknowledged their right to pass. In the parking lot, Kate led the way to her car while Gavin glanced around. They were still within the prison grounds, but he hadn't been outside the main walls of the facility since he'd been brought to Swenton. He was already beginning to feel an intoxicating sense of freedom.

Kate drove an Acura. It looked fairly new. Gavin had tried to keep up with the changes in vehicles. He was familiar with names and models but was excited to see and touch and ride in one of these sleek new cars. She unlocked the vehicle with a remote, and Gavin opened the door to get in the passenger side. As he swung his legs in, they hit the dash. "I'm sorry," Kate laughed. "I should have adjusted that earlier. Adele was the last one to ride with me; she's only five-four."

Gavin enjoyed hearing Kate laugh. He'd heard her laugh in his dreams and was pleased that she sounded exactly as he'd imagined. He reached under the seat for a lever to adjust his seat, but Kate quickly pointed to a set of buttons on the door panel. "You can move it any direction you want, even up or down. Another button adjusts the lumbar support and there's one for heat, too, if you want it."

He decided against the heat, but played with the other buttons as Kate backed the car out of the parking spot and headed toward the main gates. They stopped at the security exit, and Kate showed Gavin's paperwork to the guard before driving through.

A wave of euphoria washed over Gavin as he observed the freedom that lay before his eyes. He was still limited in many ways, but being outside the prison facility felt exhilarating! He wanted to take in every site and sound and smell that his senses could grasp, but it was almost overwhelming, so he decided to be selective. He was curious about the car itself but decided to inspect it more closely once they got on the highway. Instead, he looked around. The traffic seemed heavy. It was just past eight in the morning; everyone was probably on their way to work.

Kate looked over at him and smiled. "A little different from the last time you saw it?"

He nodded. The city had changed. The buildings were taller, the streets wider. Suddenly Gavin longed to see something he recognized. Everything was a little too different, and it left him feeling lost in a place that should be familiar.

Kate turned left, and though some of the buildings had changed, Gavin recognized the area. As they stopped at an intersection, Gavin saw a Denny's restaurant on his right. "Hey! I've been to that Denny's!" he exclaimed, pointing to the familiar restaurant. A burst of nostalgia replaced the forlorn feeling. "My friends and I used to come here sometimes. It was open twenty-four hours, so we'd hang out here after a party. We'd stay till, like, four in the morning and then drive home and sleep the whole next day."

GAVIN MCDERMOTT was still that young boy in so many ways, and Kathryn enjoyed hearing him reminisce. She was obliged to stick to their itinerary, but offered, "Next time we can stop there for breakfast if you like."

"Really?"

Kathryn smiled. She may as well have offered him the moon. It made her realize how many things she took for granted. She was glad to see small pleasures appreciated in such a big way.

"Really," she promised. "Your mom is making brunch this morning, so I thought we'd just pick up coffee and a muffin for the drive."

"At Starbucks?"

"You bet." She pulled into the drive-through, but before she placed their order, turned to Gavin. "Do you trust me?"

"Sure," he grinned.

Kathryn ordered two of her favorite drink, along with a couple of muffins. She paid and then handed one of the steaming cups to Gavin.

"This is good. I mean really good! Wow!"

She laughed. It was going to be an interesting day. Seeing so many things for the first time through Gavin's eyes was almost like experiencing it herself all over again. She thanked her Inner Being for the delightful new way of looking at life, knowing she'd be forever changed by it.

GAVIN FIDDLED with the stereo, watched the GPS screen in amazement as it guided them through the city, and adjusted his seat more than once, just because he could. He felt like a kid let loose in a department store right before Christmas. The feeling of freedom was as delicious as the latte and muffin he had just devoured. He was beginning to feel much more relaxed and even wondered what he'd been so afraid of.

"What kind of music do you like?" he asked Kate as he surfed through satellite radio channels with the remote control. The new technology was something he knew little about. Before he'd gone to prison, satellites were used by the government and the military and at most were topics in popular action movies. Now, according to Kate, Global Positioning Systems were common in new vehicles, hundreds of music channels were available by satellite, too, and remote controls came with almost every piece of equipment. Gavin liked the convenience at his fingertips. He was beginning to really like the new world he was being reintroduced to.

"I like just about everything. Well, except maybe heavy metal. But if that's your preference, go ahead," she offered graciously. "Listen to whatever you like."

Gavin was curious to learn more about her, so he probed, "You must have a preference."

"It depends on what mood I'm in; generally I like easy-listening or pop. But I want you to pick something that you want to listen to, Gavin. This is your day."

He continued searching until he found an 80s channel and recognized a favorite song. "This is great!" He closed his eyes for a moment not wanting to miss what was going on around him but enraptured by the familiar song. With the melody transporting him back in time, the words came to mind as if he'd heard them yesterday.

When he opened his eyes, they were nearing the outskirts of the city, and fields spread out before them. The countryside hadn't changed all that much. He recognized some of the farms and acreages that dotted the landscape.

"Gavin," Kate interrupted his observations. "You may experience some powerful emotions today, and I want to be able to help you through them."

"I appreciate that."

"We can take time as you experience them, or deal with them later; it's up to you. But I think it will be most beneficial to deal with them as they arise.

"I've told your parents that this kind of thing is to be expected," Kate went on. "They'll probably be dealing with their own issues, too."

"This has been hard on them. Mom said Dad's taking medication for his heart."

"It's not your fault, you know."

Gavin wanted to believe her, but he felt guilty for the pain he'd put his parents through. He didn't respond right away.

"Everyone is responsible for their own lives, Gavin. No one is a victim. Everything that happens to us is an exact match to the vibration we're offering. Everything, no exceptions. And whenever something does happen, we get to choose how we respond to it."

"No victims?" Gavin looked at her in astonishment. "I killed a man. Are you saying he wasn't a victim?" As he said the words, he questioned whether he wanted to have that particular conversation at that moment, and he realized the answer was yes. It was time.

Gavin heard Kate take a breath. She glanced his way before answering. He appreciated that she was sensitive to his feelings and hadn't pressured him to talk before he was ready.

"Yes, Gavin, that's what I'm saying. I know it's hard to grasp, but when you do, you'll see it's the only thing that makes sense. The young man that died that day… he chose to die that day...in that way." She paused to look at Gavin. "And you chose to be a part of it. It really is as simple as that."

Gavin's mind reeled with the new ideas. It was liberating in a sense, as if he'd been pardoned of his crime, yet part of him wanted to argue. That part of him was forgetting the things he'd already learned from Kate, his spirit guide. "But that's like justifying the crime—like it's all right to kill someone."

"Can you justify how it felt for you? Could you justify doing it again?"

"No!" Gavin exclaimed with a fervor that surprised him. Nevertheless, he was beginning to see what Kate was trying to say. Then he remembered what she'd already explained to him in a dream and decided to share it. "I think I know what you mean, though. I know now why I chose to have this experience."

"YOU DO?" she frowned.

"I wanted to know what freedom felt like. I wanted to experience it in such an all-encompassing way that I needed to experience complete and total bondage first to know the contrast."

Kathryn was stunned. He was absolutely right, of course; it made perfect sense. But how he'd gained such insight was a mystery.

"Gavin," she replied. "You amaze me sometimes. How do you know these things?" It was an unfair question, and she immediately regretted asking it. He was connected to the same stream of knowing that she was, and just because she was the so-called expert didn't mean she had a monopoly on wisdom. She was looking for a way to apologize when he answered with words that astonished her.

"I have dreams," he said simply.

"And you learn these things in your dreams?"

"Yeah, mostly," he said, hesitating.

Kathryn was hanging on his words. She sensed he was going to reveal what she'd been wondering about since she'd first met him, but he became quiet, and she questioned if he was ready to share it with her. Kathryn wanted to respect his need for privacy, but at the same time wanted to encourage him to trust her. She decided to pursue it.

"Gavin, you don't have to share this if you don't feel comfortable, but what you're saying isn't going to shock me. I've met and talked to people who receive information through visions, people who regularly receive channeled information, people who have spirit guides and out-of-body experiences. None of those are uncommon."

"Have you ever experienced any of that?"

I should have known he'd ask that question. She wanted to say she'd experienced it, but in truth her knowledge was mostly secondhand. She attributed her insights and understanding to a higher Source, but overall she was lacking when it came to supernatural experiences.

"No, I haven't," she said honestly. "I envy people who do, though. My husband had incredible dreams and out-of-body experiences. He used to wake me in the middle of the night to tell me the new insights he'd received. I'd love to know what that feels like, but I have to admit it scares me a little."

She knew she was treading in dangerous territory. Sharing her personal life with a patient was not a good idea, but she felt so compelled with Gavin. It was almost as if she was offering her story in exchange for his. It gave him the courage he needed to share the deeper part of him that she knew existed but couldn't draw out any other way.

GAVIN HEARD what Kate said, but couldn't help reading between the lines. "You said your husband used to do that. He doesn't anymore?"

"He...passed away nearly four years ago."

"I'm sorry." Gavin wished he could offer some sort of comfort. He could tell by the way she spoke that it was a painful subject. Four years wasn't a long time. She still wore her wedding rings and obviously still missed him.

The revelation didn't surprise him, however. He'd known, somehow, that she wasn't attached to anyone in that way. It didn't feel right thinking of her with another man. He wondered sometimes if he wasn't just hopeful, maybe even jealous, but now he knew that what he'd suspected was true.

Gavin was eager to return to their conversation; he had so much to say. He wanted to tell her everything but knew he had to withhold some of it. "I met you," he began, trusting she was familiar enough with the paranormal that she would believe him. "…before you came to Swenton."

She frowned at him. "But when…? How…?"

He wasn't sure how to describe it in a way that made sense, but he took a stab at it. "I guess it was a dream or a vision, maybe even a hallucination. I was in the infirmary…"

"Yes, I read about that in your file. You had the Srela virus."

"Yeah. Apparently I was really sick for a while. The only thing is, I don't remember any of that. All I remember are the dreams I had. Except…they didn't feel like dreams; they felt real. I met people and talked to them, learned things…only to find that none of it really happened.

"The day I got out of the infirmary…" He stopped. Suddenly the story seemed so outrageous that he wasn't even sure he believed it himself.

Kate was able to continue for him. "That was the same day I came to Swenton to speak in the auditorium," she said eagerly. "And you looked at me as if you knew me!"

"I did know you," Gavin shrugged, not sure how much to reveal and how much to hold back.

She glanced at him, a dozen questions on her face, but they both knew they would have to wait. They were nearing Redding and the turnoff to his parents' farm. He directed her as they pulled into town. They had to drive through a part of Redding before turning, and Gavin noticed that not nearly as much had changed in this smaller center as it had in the city.

Not wanting to miss a single detail, he looked intently at every building, at every face he saw on the streets, and in the cars they passed. Part of him wanted to see a familiar face, and another part hoped he wouldn't see or be seen by anyone he knew. He wasn't ready for that. Being at home with his parents was a huge step and all that he wanted for his first day out.

KATHRYN WAS CURIOUS to learn about Gavin's dreams and visions, especially now that he'd revealed she had been a part of them. It explained why he'd looked at her the way he had, and why he'd seemed so distressed that first day. It also explained the times he knew what she was going to say before she said it. It explained a lot, yet left her with a host of questions. She hoped to be able to talk about it with him soon. Maybe if all went well, they could continue the conversation on the drive home.

Now, however, Gavin was taking in every detail, and rightly so. She wanted those moments to be special for him and memorable in a good way. He had eighteen years of relatively good memories before the one that forever changed his life, and she wanted him to re-capture those memories. She wanted to help him look back at the past and selectively sift, to bring into his present focus only that which served him.

He was quiet as they drove the last stretch of the journey, and Kathryn wished she could read his mind. She was more than willing to help him through any difficult times, but she couldn't unless he shared them with her.

As they turned off the secondary highway and on to a gravel road that led to his parents' farm, Gavin let out a long, slow breath. Kathryn slowed the car and looked at him for a quick moment. She could see the emotion on his face. He was dealing with something powerful.

"Do you need a moment? Is there anything you want to deal with before we get to your farm?"

Gavin nodded. "Can we do that process again—the one where I take back my power?"

"Absolutely," Kathryn assured him. She pulled the car off to the side of the road, giving him her full attention. "What are you feeling?"

"I'm not sure," Gavin admitted. "It almost feels like the panic attacks I used to have before I knew what I was afraid of."

Kathryn wasn't familiar with any panic attacks. She hadn't read about it in his paperwork but decided to forgo asking. She could always address it in a future session. For now, she wanted to help Gavin find the dom-inant emotion and the thoughts that were fueling it.

"Does it feel like the fear we dealt with before? When you think about the dream with the shackles, does this feel the same?"

"Yes and no," Gavin replied. "I know it has to do with my parents. Since I told you about my dad being on heart medication, I've had this heavy feeling. I told you I understand the reason I chose to spend so many years in prison, but what I don't understand is why they had to suffer because of it?"

Kathryn paused a moment before she responded. It seemed a little heartless to simply tell him they had created it, although she believed that to be true. It felt like a pat answer and not what Gavin needed in that moment. Instead she tried to guide him to his own clarity. "Are you feeling guilty?"

"I think so."

"Whatever names we give those low emotions, it's important to understand the powerlessness that's associated with them. That's the reason you feel so bad right now, Gavin. Guilt is a very powerless emotion, and it's often associated with feelings of unworthiness. Why don't we try using the same analogy from your dream?"

Gavin nodded.

"It doesn't matter what *right* those feelings of guilt and unworthiness have to be in your experience. I'm sure you've been justifying them, but in doing so you're letting the emotions control you, just like the fear did. You can put an end to the dominance they've had over you. They've had you in bondage, Gavin, but it doesn't have to be that way.

"Think of the influence they had on you," she reminded him. "Feel the immense power they held. Now take that power back. Feel it flowing to you. You're in control, and you get to decide how you want to feel. The power belongs to you now. Feel it surging through you like a wave in the ocean—filling you and lifting you. It's yours now, Gavin. The power is yours to use, to create something that serves you better."

Gavin's eyes were closed, and she saw him take a deep breath. Then a look flashed across his face, indicating he was indeed feeling the power he'd reclaimed. She was thrilled to see him using and benefiting from the techniques she was teaching him. It was very rewarding.

"Did that help?" she inquired after he had opened his eyes.

"Yeah," he smiled. "I'm ready to go home now."

Chapter 12

As they pulled into the farmyard Gavin had grown up in, Kathryn noticed him taking in the familiar elements. What captured her attention, however, was the sight of his parents rushing out of the house to greet him. She'd felt the love they had for their son when she spoke to them on the phone, and she was about to see it demonstrated as they welcomed him home after nearly eighteen years. Almost before the vehicle stopped, Gavin sprang from the car and went to them. The three hugged and were soon joined by Gavin's sister and her husband.

Kathryn stood back, not wanting to intrude on the heartwarming family scene. What she witnessed next was even more touching. Two little girls joined the group, and she watched as Gavin turned to them in awe. Both parties were obviously shy, having never met. With Sandra's encouragement, the girls gave their uncle a hug, and Gavin held them in a long, loving embrace.

After a few moments Gavin's mom, Carol, turned to Kathryn, beaming a thank-you. Then she beckoned her to join them as they went inside.

Kathryn had come in a professional capacity and was quite happy to stay on the sidelines and simply observe the reunion between Gavin and his family. She'd told Carol as much. But Carol insisted that Kathryn be treated as family who, she found out, received the grandest treatment of all. That meant not just joining them for meals but also partaking in conversation and being filled in on all that Carol, her husband, and daughter believed Kathryn ought to know about their family history.

Kathryn was surprised and somewhat moved by the love and openness she felt in Gavin's home. It differed dramatically from her own family dynamic, which was pretty much nonexistent. It was refreshing to see a family unit functioning as it was meant to function, loving and supporting and accepting one another. It was as if they had never been separated by years or prison bars.

After a spread of sausage, eggs, pancakes, fried potatoes—everything, she discovered, that Gavin loved—they all sat back full and satisfied.

The little girls were completely taken with their newfound uncle, having only seen pictures and heard stories of the man. Gavin was a natural with kids. He bounced them on his knee and teased them. He asked about their friends, their toys, and their favorite television shows.

With the mention of television, Gavin looked at his father. "I hear you got the new TV hooked up; I can't wait to see it."

As the three men headed to the basement with the kids in tow, Kathryn turned to Carol. "I'd be happy to do the dishes. I want you to have as much time with Gavin as possible."

"We'll let the men have a few minutes to themselves," Carol said, clearing plates from the dining-room table. "But you can help if you like; it'll be nice to get to know you better."

As they cleaned up, Kathryn felt increasingly at ease with the McDermott women. They asked about her home, her family, and her job. By the time the dishes were washed and put away, Kathryn was quite sure that they knew more about her than her own family did.

It was an odd feeling. She wanted to maintain her professional image yet felt more like a "friend" that Gavin had brought home to meet the family. She decided to put a stop to it, although it felt good in ways she didn't understand, and began to talk about Gavin from a professional standpoint. "Gavin's doing very well in the program," she informed them. "I'm very happy with his progress."

"What do you hope to accomplish with the men you work with?" Sandra asked casually. "Generally, I mean. What are your goals with the program?"

"The main goal is to help them get in touch with their emotions, to give them tools in dealing with the kinds of huge emotional issues that can arise in their situations, and to help them see themselves in a new light. I work a lot with their self-image."

"Wow, helping men connect with their emotions..." Sandra shook her head. "That's a tall order. Can I make an appointment for my husband?"

They all laughed. Being with these women was comfortable; Kathryn felt like they were old friends.

"So Gavin is in touch with his emotions? How does he feel about what happened?"

She knew Carol was referring to the crime Gavin had committed, although Kathryn doubted they had ever used the word *criminal,* let alone *murder.* She understood their reasoning. They were wisely choosing how they wanted to see Gavin all those years, and it had served them well.

"He's feeling guilty." Kathryn decided to divulge some of what Gavin had shared without crossing the line of patient/counselor confidentiality. "...for a life ending, obviously. But he's dealing with guilt, too, for what he feels he put you through."

"Oh, Kathryn, he doesn't need to be carrying that load—not with everything else he has to deal with!" Carol exclaimed. "I had no idea he was feeling that way about us.

"I'm glad you told me, though," she patted Kathryn's hand in a motherly gesture. "I'd like to talk to him about that."

"He's had some spiritual experiences, too, and has developed a significant connection to a higher power. He learns things through dreams and visions. I feel that it's a very positive thing for him."

"I've wondered about that," Carol replied. "He's asked me about God. We've had several conversations through letters or in person when I've visited. I told him what I believe, but I don't expect him to follow the way of the church, necessarily. I've always believed he'd find God in his own way, in his own time."

Carol's attitude, her outlook on life and on spiritual matters, impressed Kathryn. It was no wonder that Gavin had such a strong foundation from which to grow. It explained a lot.

"I hope you're not telling Kate any embarrassing stories about me," Gavin interrupted their discussion by coming up behind his mom, giving her a bear hug and a kiss on the cheek. "My therapy is going well. I don't want to have to go back and relive the time in kindergarten when Jeremy Conner and his friends painted my hair bright pink with tempera paints."

"Well, now, maybe you should. How do you feel about that, Gavin?" Kathryn entreated, pretending to be serious.

Gavin laughed, and Kathryn noticed a sparkle in his eyes she hadn't seen before. It was happiness, obviously. He was home and for the next few hours free. It suited him.

"If you'll stop being my shrink for a bit," he smiled at Kathryn, "I'll show you around the farm." He looked at the rest of his family. "Anybody else feel like going for a walk?"

The little girls wanted to join them, and Gavin's dad accepted the invitation, telling Gavin he wanted to show him improvements he'd made around the place. The others opted to stay indoors.

The property was just an acreage now, the farmland having been sold since Gavin's dad retired a few years earlier. He had a new shop he wanted to show Gavin. Kathryn and the children followed, interested in the tour as well.

The youngest girl was about five or six and the older one around nine, Kathryn guessed. They were adorable and talkative. The youngest took Kathryn's hand as they walked. She eagerly told her about the tire swing her grandpa had made for them. Kathryn felt a slight longing, as she occasionally did around children. She had hoped to have children of her own one day, but those hopes were dashed. She had long since dealt with the emotions and now just wanted to be present in the moment.

The shop was impressive, fully equipped with power tools, gardening tools, a little garden tractor with a tiny matching utility trailer, and a workbench with neatly ordered hand tools hanging above it. The heated building was complete with a washroom, a fridge that had probably sat in their kitchen when Gavin was a child, and an older style coffee maker. And, Gavin pointed out laughing, it had become the new home of the ancient but still working television that had lost its place in the house. It was undoubtedly his father's favorite place to spend his days.

Kathryn watched Gavin examine several of the power tools. She knew he was familiar with wood-working, having studied his files, but he never talked about it in their sessions. He complimented his dad on the impressive collection, and then the group went outside again.

It was an ideal day, delightfully warm for spring-time, although a patch or two of snow still spotted the ground. Gavin seemed to want to continue looking around. When his dad returned to the house, and the children ran off to play, Gavin turned to Kathryn. "Do you want to see more?"

"Sure," she smiled, happy to see Gavin in good spirits and relaxed in his element. If he was experiencing any more negative emotion from this trip down memory lane, it wasn't evident on his face.

She'd already noticed he had a very handsome face, easy on the eyes, and a body that a stone carver might fashion a Greek god after. Kathryn appreciated the view. She was, after all, a woman and not yet past the age of appreciating a good male body when she had the pleasure of observing one. However, she kept her observations stored away in a private place she rarely let herself go to. It was something she knew she shouldn't be indulging in, especially with one of her students, so she silently reprimanded herself.

She truly hoped that Gavin would find someone to love; he deserved it. It had to be someone who could appreciate him for all he was and accept him, his past included. She suspected that he would want children of his own one day, too. That seemed like a lot to ask, but Kathryn believed he would find the right woman. He was still young, and he had so much to offer.

GAVIN WAS REMINDED of the images from his vision the night before. Kate was walking with him as he showed her the farm; they were alone, and he longed to take her hand just as he'd imagined. He longed to talk more about the topic they'd begun in the car.

They walked past the large garden plot behind the house. The soil had been prepared for the upcoming planting season, and perennials were coming to life in the unseasonably warm weather. His father had done quite a bit of landscaping in recent years, leveling the sloping bank from the house to the ravine below. Now flagstone steps led from one grassy level to another. Although covered with patches of snow, the yard had a park-like feel.

Gavin stood aside, allowing Kate to go before him on the first set of steps. As she turned to him with a polite smile, he instinctively knew what was about to happen. He grabbed her hand in time to catch her as she slipped and with his other hand, steadied her. She'd reached for his arm when she began to fall, and now the two stood grasping one another.

"I'm sorry," Kate laughed uneasily. "I wasn't paying attention. The melting snow must have made the stones slippery." She righted herself and quickly took her hand off Gavin's arm. He let go of her hand but continued to steady her with his other hand on her shoulder. As she took a step he noticed her grimace in pain, so he reached for her hand again.

"I think I've twisted my ankle." She looked up at him weakly.

"Let me help you to the house," he offered. "Sandy's a nurse; she can have a look at it."

Chapter 13

Kathryn had no choice but to lean on Gavin as he helped her to the house. He'd offered to carry her, which he could have done effortlessly, but she insisted she could walk. It felt strange and awkward with his arm around her waist, and her hand on his shoulder. Strange because it had been so long since she'd felt a man's arm around her, and awkward because part of her liked the feelings of warmth and closeness it produced. She was relieved when the rest of the family rushed to her aid.

They helped her inside, and once they were in the living room, Sandra examined the ankle. "It's not broken," she said confidently. "It's a pretty bad sprain, though. Gavin, can you get an ice pack from the freezer?"

Kathryn was annoyed at herself for being so careless. She'd planned to be a silent observer, letting Gavin be the man of the hour, and now everyone was gathered around, tending to her needs.

Gavin's father, assuming responsibility for her mishap, had already apologized more than once for the condition of the steps. Sandra elevated Kathryn's foot and wrapped the ice pack around it with a towel. Carol offered food and drink, painkillers, and extra pillows for comfort.

Kathryn looked at Gavin, who was standing back watching her. She gestured a helpless, "I'm sorry."

He sat down across from her and leaned forward. "How does it feel, Kate?" he mocked playfully. "Do you want to talk about it?"

She had to laugh at the way he'd turned the tables. Now she was the patient, and he was asking questions about her well-being.

"Embarrassing," she shook her head. "I can't believe I did that. I'm not usually such a klutz."

"I really think you should deal with that negative emotion," he teased.

"I'll be fine," she replied, putting a stop to his little game. "But thanks anyway."

Not put off by her reproof, he sat watching her. She saw something in his eyes she hadn't noticed before, but she wasn't sure what it was. Concern, maybe. The rest of the family finally sat down, and Kathryn hoped the attention would now be diverted from her.

"So how often will Gavin be allowed to come home?" Sandra asked Kathryn.

"Every two weeks, for now. It should change to once a week by summer."

"We really appreciate you doing this for Gavin," Carol added.

Gavin shot a look her way, and Kathryn could tell that he wanted to respond to his mom's comment. She even knew what he was about to say.

"Mom, Kate's been teaching me some amazing stuff. It's our thoughts that cause things to happen in our lives. Kate didn't do this. I mean, she played a part in it, but it couldn't have happened if I hadn't been vibrationally ready."

Carol listened to her son's explanation, but it was obvious that what she was hearing was new to her.

"Our minds are powerful. We create what we think about. I know why I created this experience. I understand it now." He stopped, allowing his family to take in his words. "Do you remember what I was like..." He looked at each of them. "Before I went to prison?"

"I'm not sure what you mean?" His mother had a blank look on her face.

"I was like a car revved up to go with the breaks on. I wanted to experience life so badly, but it seemed as if everything was holding me back. I was a wild cat, caged up. I was angry at life, too; I couldn't understand what was happening to me. In some ways I was already a prisoner. I wanted to know what it was like to be truly free, and now I'm finding out in a way that most people can't imagine."

Carol dabbed at her eyes as she listened to her son speak. His father, also moved by Gavin's acknowledgment, cleared his throat.

Gavin's insight continued to wow Kathryn. He was beyond her, spiritually. She'd thought about it before, but now as she listened to this young man, wise beyond his years, she wondered how much more she would be able to teach him, how much more value she would be to him. She felt sad at the thought of their sessions ending. The day would come; it was inevitable. Now it seemed closer than she'd anticipated, and she suddenly wished she could find a way to remain in Gavin's life. Hers had already been changed dramatically just by knowing him.

CAROL LOOKED AT HER SON, love and pride radiating from her face. "That makes so much sense, sweetheart. It can apply to us, then, too. We chose to be a part of this. And you know, I can honestly say I don't regret it. My faith in God is stronger than ever. I look at people differently now. I'm more open and accepting. And," she smiled, "I have a son that I couldn't be more proud of."

Gavin felt his own tears well up at his mother's praise. Love and acceptance he had received and was truly grateful for, but pride was something he hadn't dared to wish for. He was moved beyond words.

Sandra echoed her mother's sentiment. "We're all proud of you, Gavin. What you've gone through…I can't begin to imagine. And now…" She was nearing tears as well. "You're just such an amazing human being."

Gavin couldn't speak; emotion was all but choking him. All around him was an outpouring of love.

Even Kate had a look on her face he had never seen before. It was love; he could feel it, but he was quite sure she wouldn't define it as that. To her it probably felt like pride in his accomplishments or joy in being part of this reunion. But she'd know soon enough. He was confident of that. He'd seen it, and he believed in his visions.

Carol stood up and announced, "Well, I guess we have a schedule to keep. You two will have to be heading back to the city before long, and I want to set out a bite to eat before you go." She stopped by Gavin's chair and stroked his face lovingly. She still had tears in her eyes.

Gavin knew that showing emotion had been hard for his mom at one time, but she'd learned to do it. His father on the other hand—although kind, loving, and soft spoken—seemed extremely uncomfortable with displays of emotion. He'd always known how his father felt. A pat on the back, an unexpected gift—those were the kinds of things that disclosed his dad's true feelings, and Gavin respected him for that.

He watched as his father stood to his feet and cleared his throat again, probably to remove the lump rather than speak. He patted Gavin's shoulder and mumbled, "I have to...um...check on something out in the shop; can you let me know when supper's ready?" With that, he walked out of the room.

Sandra's husband had taken the girls downstairs after Kate's mishap, and they were still there watching a movie. Sandra stood up, leaving Gavin and Kate sitting. She addressed them before walking out. "I'm going to help mom with the food. Kate, you stay put," she instructed. "Gavin, you keep her company."

Gavin raised his hand in mock salute to his older sister as she left the room. It was more for Kate's amusement than anything else, because Sandra's back was to him. When he turned to Kate, she was smiling, and he saw the same look in her eyes that he'd observed a few minutes earlier.

"How's your ankle?" he inquired. "Does it hurt?"

"I can't feel anything with the ice on it," she replied. "I think it'll be fine. Thanks for catching me, by the way. I might have done a lot more damage if you hadn't."

"My pleasure," Gavin replied, remembering how wonderful it had been to hold Kate in his arms. He felt such an outflowing of love for her in that moment that he decided to share something else. "I kind of saw it happen."

"I SHOULDN'T BE SURPRISED, Gavin," she laughed, "but I am. Tell me what you saw, and when."

"It's kind of hard to explain; I mean...it happened so quickly. In my dream last night, I was holding your hand. And today, just before you tripped, I knew it was going to happen, so I grabbed your hand without thinking."

"You dreamed you were holding my hand? I don't understand." Something strange was going on, and Kathryn was very much a part of it. Gavin had an odd look on his face; there was something he wasn't saying. "You didn't see me slip last night, did you?"

"No," he admitted. "I saw us walking in the garden."

Her discomfort began to increase. "What else have you seen in your visions?"

"Kate," he said, sounding like the teacher, while she definitely felt like the student. "It would take days to tell you everything. I'm not sure now's the right time."

"I can respect that," she conceded. "But Gavin, something is happening that I don't understand. I'll be the first to admit I don't know everything, but the things I've seen in you...they're beyond what I've observed in anyone else I've worked with; it leaves me feeling...a little daunted."

"I don't want you to feel that way, Kate. You're helping me so much. I don't want that to change."

"It doesn't have to change, Gavin," she assured him. "We can deal with whatever you're experiencing. I'm sorry for implying it's your fault in any way.

"You know," she added quickly, wanting to repair the rift she may have caused. "I have no doubt that we're meant to learn from each other. I've already learned so much from you. I wanted to tell you before that I'm proud of you, too. You are an amazing human being, just like Sandra said."

"SUPPER'S READY," Carol announced. "We're going to eat casual, though. I've set everything on the table. We can all fill our plates and join Kate here in the living room. Gavin, can you go and call your father? Kate, I'll dish a plate for you. What would you like? I've got cold sliced turkey and ham, brown or white buns, cheese..."

Gavin knew that Kate was in good hands. His mom thrived on helping people, fussing over them. He laughed to himself as he went to the shop to get his dad. He found him oiling a wooden object with a rag.

"What are you making, Dad?"

"It's a picture frame. Your mother wanted to give Kate a little something for…you know…her part in this," he explained uneasily. "She has a picture of the four of us taken at your last birthday. So I made a frame to go with it."

Gavin took it from his father and examined it. "It's great, Dad. Is this burled walnut?"

"Yup," he replied. "Tough as nails to work with, but it sure polishes up nice."

"It's beautiful," Gavin replied, rubbing his hand over the smooth oiled surface of the distinctively patterned wood. "I'm sure Kate will love it."

"She's a nice girl," his father submitted. It sounded more like a suggestion than a statement, and Gavin had to smile.

"Yeah, she's great."

They walked back to the house, and no more words passed between them. Gavin respected how hard it was for his father to communicate his feelings, and he decided not to make things more uncomfortable by telling him how much he loved him, but he wanted to. More than that, he needed to. It could wait, however. He'd find the right moment.

The rest of the afternoon faded away quickly, and too soon it was time for goodbyes. He and Kate had to leave, but Gavin didn't feel regret; he'd had a thoroughly enjoyable day, and he knew there would be more to come.

Everyone hugged both him and Kate, and tears flowed again. This time he noticed Kate wipe away a tear as she thanked his parents for the lovely gift. Gavin longed to hug her, too. He wanted to thank her for the incredible day, thank her for being a part of it, but it didn't seem appropriate when she was leaving with him. Besides, they still had two hours together on the drive back.

He helped her to the car. She insisted she was able to drive. It was her left foot, and she could rest it as she drove. Gavin admired her spunk. She'd been through a lot in her life and seemed all the stronger for it. He sensed she was lonely though and wished he could help ease that for her. He was quiet with his thoughts as she drove the first stretch of the trip back. He wanted to tell her so much but knew that the time wasn't right. He closed his eyes, finding the relief it brought. He'd hardly slept in the past twenty-four hours and was suddenly feeling the effects of it.

WITH THE DAY'S EVENTS still fresh, Kathryn let her mind sift through the overabundance of thoughts and feelings that had arisen. It felt like more than ten hours ago that she and Gavin had driven through Swenton's gates; so much had happened. She wanted to talk more about the subject that had come up but after his comment, didn't want to push it. She had to respect his silence if that's what he needed.

Kathryn glanced over at him, wondering what he was thinking, and was surprised to find him sleeping. She smiled. *He mentioned he hadn't slept much last night; he must be exhausted. Maybe it's just as well.* She couldn't help but speculate about what he'd seen in his visions, why he'd been holding her hand in the garden and why he was hesitant to share any more of it.

Although she truly hoped that he hadn't developed romantic feelings for her, she suspected it was the case. Kathryn was quite sure now that's what she'd seen in his eyes, and she felt responsible. She hadn't been as careful as she'd been taught in relating to a patient.

Of course, he hadn't actually said it, and she had no way of knowing for certain what he'd seen in his visions, but for a moment she allowed herself to think about it. *What if he's fallen in love with me? It's ridiculous of course. He's six years younger than I am. I just happen to be the first woman he's had any direct association with in seventeen years. Plus I've been part of some major emotional breakthroughs in his life. He's demonstrating obvious symptoms of transference.*

Addressing it would require tactfulness and sensitivity. It was something that had never come up in all Kathryn's years of practice, but she had a colleague who had dealt with it and could give her advice.

She looked at Gavin for a moment. He seemed peaceful and relaxed after what had appeared to be a satisfying day. He'd been happy, and the exchange with his parents had been not only heartwarming to watch, but therapeutic for all involved. They were truly a remarkable family. Kathryn was honored to know them and be welcomed into their midst, even feel like one of them. She'd let herself be drawn into their warmth, and it was incredibly fulfilling. She hadn't felt that in a long, long time.

She thought of Gavin's touch and the feelings he had evoked in her that afternoon. Those were feelings she hadn't felt in a long time as well. *It's not Gavin,* she reasoned. *It could have happened with any man. He was just the first man to touch me like that since Kevin died. Not to mention he's an amazing physical specimen. A body like that is bound to effect any living, breathing woman.* She glanced his way again.

All it means is that I'm ready to think about dating again, she concluded, realizing for the first time that she may have been wrong hiding herself away from men for so long. The subject was still a little painful, but she knew she had to open herself up to it. *If I don't,* she analyzed. *I could fall prey to this kind of temptation.*

As terrific as Gavin is, I'm not the right woman for him, she continued, justifying her decision. *He might not be able to see that, but I can. Everyone else would see it, too. He needs someone his age, someone to settle down and have children with.*

Gavin sighed audibly and twisted in his seat, trying to get more comfortable. Kathryn didn't want to wake him but knew he'd rest better if his seat back was lowered. She leaned across, but the button on his door was just beyond her reach, so she adjusted herself and glanced over a second time. Leaning further, she pushed it quickly so she could concentrate on driving again.

A car horn quickly brought her attention back to the road, and she swerved in time to miss the car that she had veered toward. As she did, her car hit a patch of icy snow and careened out of control. She tried to bring it back, but the vehicle continued in the direction of the steep ditch that flanked the highway.

Suddenly she felt herself being thrown, her seatbelt the only thing keeping her from being tossed about the vehicle. The car was moving through the air; they were rolling. It hit down once, bounced, and rolled again. The roof crumpled in, and she crouched as close to the steering wheel as she could.

It seemed to be happening in slow motion. At one point, she looked over at Gavin. Eyes still groggy with sleep, he reached out to her. She heard him say her name, but it sounded like an echo, as if he was a distance away.

They finally landed against something solid, and she felt her body lurch forward, colliding with the airbag as it exploded. The impact sent her head rebounding back, tearing at the muscles in her neck. The car instantly filled with an acrid stench, and she turned away from it. As she did, she noticed that Gavin's eyes were closed and his body limp. Blood gushed from a cut on his forehead. She called his name and reached out to touch his face. She gently shook him, calling his name again. When he opened his eyes, a smile slowly formed on his face. Kathryn immediately let out a sigh as relief filled her being. "Are you okay?"

"Yeah," he smiled again. He wasn't moving, and blood was pouring out quicker than ever. She noticed blood on his shirt, too, and put her hand on his chest to see what the source was. He lifted his hand and put it over hers.

"We have to get you to a hospital!"

"It's going to be all right, Kate."

She pulled her hand away and grabbed her purse to find her cell phone, but its contents had spilled on the floor. As she reached down to find the phone, Gavin touched her shoulder.

"It's going to be all right, Kate," he repeated.

She looked at him again and saw a light in his eyes. The light drew her, mesmerizing and terrifying her at the same time.

"You're hurt," she argued desperately. "We have to get you to the hospital."

"I had a great time today, Kate." He was obviously delusional, talking as if nothing was wrong when everything that could possibly be wrong, was. "There's something I wanted to tell you."

"Shhh. Don't try to talk now, Gavin."

"I love you, Kate."

"Gavin… I…"

"I love you," he repeated.

His face held the evidence to support his words. Tears filled her eyes; she had no idea how to respond. He was hurt, maybe even seriously. He was delusional, saying things he might regret. Nevertheless, she had to answer him, and only one response seemed acceptable. "I love you too, Gavin."

He stroked her face and smiled. "It's going to be all right, Kate."

Stop saying that! she implored silently. It only served to confirm her belief that things were really, really not all right. The side of his face was covered with blood. She attempted to wipe it, but he wouldn't let her. He took her hand and kissed it, then looked into her eyes and smiled again.

Kathryn wanted to kiss him—if only to give him reason to live. She was afraid he was dying, and she knew that it was all her fault. "Gavin…." She began to cry. He pulled her to him, their lips uniting. She gave herself fully to the kiss, not caring about the consequences, not caring about anything except that Gavin live. His lips felt incredibly tender and warm. As long as he was kissing her back, she knew he was all right. She wanted him to be all right. She desperately needed him to be all right, because she couldn't deny it any longer; she was in love with him, too.

Part 3

~Kate~

Every person, all the events of your life are there because you have drawn them there. What you choose to do with them is up to you.

—RICHARD BACH

Chapter 14

Kathryn opened her eyes and quickly shut them again. The light was too much to take; it was almost painful. Curiosity made her try again. She didn't recognize what she'd seen in the quick glance, and she wondered where she was.

She opened them tentatively, squinting, and this time recognized her surroundings—not because she'd seen them before, but because the setting looked like a hospital room. As her eyes adjusted to the light, she took in more around her. It was definitely a hospital room; a nurse was rushing to her side.

Searching her mind, she tried to remember what had happened and why she was lying in a hospital bed. The nurse was speaking to her, and Kathryn had to concentrate to make out her words. She was saying Kathryn's name, asking her what she could see and if she knew where she was. Kathryn shook her head. Other than knowing a hospital room when she saw one, she had no idea where she was or why she was there.

Another nurse joined them, and a doctor came in asking more questions. When asked if she knew her full name, she answered, remembering clearly that she was Kathryn Harding.

"Kathryn, do you know what happened to you?"

She frowned. It was still a blank.

"You were in a car accident, Kathryn."

Suddenly a scene flashed into her mind. She saw the car she was heading toward, felt her own car swerve and roll…and then she remembered. "Gavin?" she asked, terrified of what the answer might be.

The doctor's brow creased. "I'm sorry, Kathryn, I'm not sure who Gavin is. But your friends and family—people who love you—have been here to visit. They're being notified that you're awake. I'm sure they'll be eager to see you."

She was utterly confused. *Why would my friends and family be glad I'm awake? How long have I been asleep? And why doesn't he know about Gavin?*

"Gavin was in the car with me. He was hurt," she started to explain and then began to cry. "I was afraid he was dying. Is he…?" She couldn't finish the sentence.

The doctor still had a slight frown on his face, but he tried to reassure her. "Kathryn, it's natural to experience confusion when you come out of a coma. It may take a day or two for you to piece everything together. You may have some temporary memory loss, but that's common in your situation. It's nothing to worry about."

"A coma," Kathryn repeated slowly. "How long?"

"It's been six weeks."

The news ought to have shocked her, but she still desperately wanted answers. "But Gavin was in the car…"

"Kathryn," he shook his head. "No one was with you. You were alone in the car."

GAVIN WENT THROUGH the motions. He ate and slept and worked, but he was feeling more discouraged by the day. He had truly wanted to believe what he'd seen and learned, but now he was having a hard time justifying any of it—the hardest part being that he had no one to confide in. He hadn't told a soul what he'd experienced when he was in the infirmary, and that was weeks ago.

At first the dreams and the teaching had comforted him. He'd hoped it might be an indication of things to come, but now he was beginning to think that it was nothing more than a hallucination, a result of the virus he'd contracted.

His family noticed the change in him. His mom was concerned and had tried to talk about it. He wanted to confide in her, but he didn't know where to start.

The hardest part was that the incident had awoken all kinds of desires in him. Before that, he'd been content to wait out the remainder of his sentence. It was nearing the end, and other than serious concerns about what it would be like on the outside, he hadn't been doing too badly.

But now he'd gotten a glimpse of what *could* be. He'd dreamed of an enchanting woman, even fallen in love, and he couldn't imagine being with anyone else. He'd learned things that made so much sense, things he couldn't dismiss. It was as if this experience had taken him to a new place, altered him in such a profound way, that he couldn't go back, yet he wasn't sure how to move forward.

He'd tried to learn more about Kate Harding and her teachings. He wanted to learn more, too, about the supernatural experience he'd had. The prison was connected with the local public library, and he could request books. Unfortunately, it often took weeks to received them, and what he'd read so far only confused him more.

He'd been informed that the parole board would be interviewing him the following week, and he assumed that if approved he would be eligible for day passes. He knew he ought to feel excited about the prospect of getting out, even if only for twelve hours at a time, but it was causing him a great deal of anxiety. In truth, he'd been feeling it for months now. It was probably normal, considering he'd spent half his life behind bars, but he didn't know how to deal with it, and it was starting to wear him down.

Finally, after much deliberation, he decided to submit a request to the prison administration. He needed to talk to someone about the way he was feeling. He knew it was a long shot. He knew he was probably delusional. Still, he let himself imagine that that person might just turn out to be Kate.

KATHRYN EXAMINED what she believed had taken place the day of the accident. Her memories felt so fresh, so real, yet hospital staff was telling her that what she thought she'd experienced was incorrect.

The person she wanted to talk to the most was her best friend. Having been informed that Kathryn had awoken from her coma, Adele was now on her way to the hospital. Adele would know about Gavin. They had discussed his progress throughout the program, and undoubtedly she'd know why Kathryn was so sure he'd been with her on that ill-fated day.

She could remember it clearly: the first day pass, Gavin's excitement and nervousness, meeting his delightful family, the walk in the garden, the sprained ankle, the trip home, and then—the most deeply imprinted memory of all—the kiss.

How could I have imagined all that? And what's become of Gavin? I'm assuming he's still in prison. Kathryn longed to see him. She knew it must be hard on him too, their sessions having ended so abruptly.

Then she thought of something else. *If that day didn't happen as I remembered, then what did happen? Did Gavin really profess his feelings for me, or was it just something I imagined? Did my own feelings for him get out of hand? If that's the case, I have some work to do. How could I have fallen in love with a patient anyway?*

She remembered her thoughts as she drove back to the city that day. Right before the accident, she'd concluded that she needed to be open to the idea of dating again, that she was indeed vulnerable around someone like Gavin.

How could I be so foolish?

Knowing what her work was, she silently made a plan. *First I need to remember what happened that day and then…*she sighed. *I have to put my feelings for Gavin in perspective. I have to deal with those romantic notions and remind myself it's just the idea of being with someone again that's so appealing.*

It was more than that. She knew now that she wanted someone like Gavin for a partner. It wasn't just that he was irresistibly attractive, physically; he was attractive in other ways. She'd never met anyone, although her husband had come close, who had so totally bewitched her with their personality in such a short time. Meeting Gavin had awoken desires that were all but dead and buried, and for that she should be thankful.

It seemed likely, now as she thought about it, that the whole thing was completely one sided. *If he was never with me outside the prison, then I have no reason to believe he felt anything for me,* she concluded, feeling disappointed. *There may not be any issues of transference to deal with at all. Of course, when I meet with him again, I'll know.* She was confident she could read him, and at that point she could decide what steps to take in continuing her work with him.

His file had likely come up before the parole board by now. She wondered if he'd gone home to see his family yet and how the experience had been for him. She was sorry she hadn't been there to share it with him, sure that it would have been as exciting for him as she'd imagined.

Kathryn was eager to see Gavin again, and that made her realize that time would be her ally. She obviously had feelings for him that she needed to deal with, not to mention the evocative memories now etched in her mind—memories she wished she could erase.

THE PRISON GRANTED Gavin's request, and he had an appointment to see someone that afternoon. He hoped Kate might miraculously appear before him, but also braced himself for the very real probability that it would be someone else. In any case, he wanted to talk about his concerns and discuss the issues he'd been stressing over. As he walked into the room, he was disappointed to see an older grey-haired man hold out his hand to welcome him. Listening to the man recite his credentials, he was reminded of how Kate had introduced herself in the prison auditorium.

Suddenly he had an idea, and he honed it while the man asked questions. Gavin answered them briefly and shared his concerns about getting out of prison, but the man was less than helpful with his replies. Compared to what Kate had already taught him, this man's advice was seriously lacking.

Just before his time was up, he asked as casually as he could, "Have you heard of a woman named Kate Harding? I…um…read about her," Gavin lied, "and I'm interested in her teaching."

The man looked blank for a moment, and then his face lit up. "You mean Kathryn Harding. Of course," he replied. "Kathryn's work—I should say her husband's work—is renowned. It's being taught in universities."

"Do you think it might be possible to see her?" Gavin asked, his mind miles ahead.

"I doubt that, son; she was in a bad car accident awhile back. It was pretty serious. Last I heard, she was still in a coma."

"Sorry to hear that," Gavin shook his head, trying to hide his reaction to the disheartening news.

"I'm familiar with the teaching of course," the man asserted. "To be honest, though, I tend to side with the critics on some of what she advocates. We could talk about it if you like."

"Oh, that's all right. What you've said today has helped me a lot," Gavin replied, stretching the truth. His counseling hadn't helped at all, but the information he'd offered regarding Kate, upsetting as it was, had put everything into a new perspective.

"Well, I'm glad I could help. I'd be happy to meet with you again if you have more concerns."

"Thank you." Gavin shook his hand, glad to be done with the meeting. His mind overflowing with ideas, he couldn't wait to put his newly formed plan into action.

KATHRYN CRIED WITH DELIGHT as her friend entered the room. Adele ran to her, and the two embraced.

"I was so afraid for you," Adele admitted after they'd both dried their tears. "I sat here every day for weeks, talking to you, praying. They didn't know if you'd make it at first."

Kathryn wasn't aware that her condition had been so serious; the hospital staff hadn't said much—other than it might take a few days for her full memory to return. She was eager for that to happen; she didn't like the confusion she was currently experiencing or her inability to recall the "actual" details of the accident.

"How are you?"

"I feel...fine," Kathryn replied. "I just can't remember everything."

"That's probably normal. What did the doctor say?" Adele asked eagerly. "How long will you have to stay in the hospital?"

"Another week, maybe longer." She responded to her friend's inquiry, but Kathryn's mind was on the things she so badly wanted to know. She hoped Adele could solve the mystery.

"Adele, I can't stop thinking about Gavin," she confessed. Kathryn was willing to talk about her feelings with her best friend, knowing she could help. "I really got attached, I guess, and I can't help but wonder how he's doing now. Did you take over any of my students? How is the program going, anyway?"

Adele stared at her for a moment, looking confused. "Kathryn," she shook her head. "I'm sorry...I have no idea what you're talking about. Who is Gavin, and what program?"

Hot coals began to sizzle in the pit of Kathryn's stomach. She knew Adele wasn't joking by the look on her face, but she couldn't understand why her friend and colleague would deny knowing about Gavin or about the program she'd been such an integral part of.

Kathryn had to fight back tears as she repeated slowly and carefully, "The prison rehabilitation program. We started it weeks before the accident. Of the ten men I counseled, Gavin was the first to be granted a temporary pass. I was with him the day of the accident...at least...I thought I was...they told me I was alone in the car."

Adele grasped Kathryn's hands and stared at her intently before speaking. Then she shook her head sadly. "I don't know what to say, sweetie," she shrugged. "We didn't get approval for the program, but don't worry; we can try again." She smiled, trying to brighten both their moods. "They can't say no forever."

"But…" Kathryn could hardly speak; every word seemed to catch in her throat. "We started it…the rehab program…we started it at Swenton. We got the approval. Dave and Norm, you and I...we started working with the inmates. We were making great progress. Gavin…"

Adele closed her eyes, but several tears escaped. She continued to hold Kathryn's hand as she shook her head again. "I'm so sorry Kathryn; none of that happened."

Chapter 15

Kathryn Harding did exist. It was little to go on, but it was the evidence Gavin needed to prove—to himself at least—that he wasn't crazy after all. It definitely lifted his spirits, although thinking of her lying in a hospital bed, seriously injured, pained him.

*I've come this far; I have to stay positive. She'll be all right. She came to me for a reason and now...*He wanted to believe she could be a part of his life one day.

Intent to carry out his plan, he went to use the phone to call his sister. "Sandy," he said, pleased at the sound of her voice, "I'm glad I caught you at home."

"Hey, Gavin! It's good to hear from you. Mom said you might be getting out on a day pass. Is that true? Have you heard anything yet?" The elation in her voice was clear.

"No, I meet with the board in a couple of days."

"Are you excited?"

"Yeah, and nervous—terrified actually. But I'll deal with it," he laughed, downplaying the topic. He wanted to ask a favor of his sister. "Can you do something for me; do you have a minute?"

"Sure Gavin, anything," she responded lovingly. "What do you need?"

"Are you by your computer?"

"I was just checking my e-mail."

"Can you search something for me?"

"Yeah, what is it?"

"It's a name...Kathryn Harding." Gavin could hear the clicking of the keys as he waited for her reply.

"The name comes up on quite a few different sites. What do you want to know about her? Who is she anyway?"

"She's a psychologist. I heard about the work she's doing, and I wanted to learn more about it."

Sandra read what she found about Kathryn, the research she and her husband had done, and the program she was trying to establish in prisons. "It says here that her husband died a few years ago," Sandra continued. "There's mention of an accident, but I'm confused…it sounds like *she* was in an accident."

"She was, not long ago. Can you find anything about that?"

Gavin listened as his sister read from a newspaper article she found. It told the city and hospital that Kathryn was in, the date of her accident, and details that Gavin would rather not have heard.

"Apparently she's been in a coma, and the doctors aren't sure if she has any permanent damage. That's too bad," Sandra added." It sounds like she was doing really good work."

"Yeah," Gavin agreed. "I thought so, too."

"I can research more if you like," Sandra offered. "...about what she teaches. I'll print it off and give it to you next time I stop by."

Gavin appreciated his sister's help. She'd been supportive over the years, and they'd become close. She visited regularly, too. It had helped him cope, survive even, knowing his family was there for him.

He thanked her and moved on to the next part of his plan. Now that he knew what city and hospital Kate was in, he called to see if they would give out any information. As he inquired, saying he was an acquaintance of Ms. Harding's, he was put through to the ward she was on.

"Ms. Harding has come out of her coma," a woman's voice informed him. "I don't have the authority to give out further information, but you can leave a message for her if you like."

"Oh...I," he stuttered, realizing he hadn't thought out his little scheme carefully enough. "I don't want to bother her." He was about to apologize and hang up but at the last minute decided to leave his name.

He hung up the phone, astounded at what he had just done. *She'll have no idea who I am, of course. But if I ever get to meet her in the future,* he justified, *I can say I'm the Gavin that inquired about her.* It was a connection, and it felt good.

He went over the information he'd acquired. She was no longer in a coma and was obviously able to receive messages; that was a good sign, although she may have suffered other injuries in the accident. She was well known, or at least her late husband was for the work he had done. That in itself was interesting news; she was a widow. Gavin hadn't given much thought to her marital status. Even though she wore wedding rings, it didn't seem to be a barrier between them in his dreams.

He wondered what it all meant. It was clear that he was being a bit obsessive in his quest. He had no idea what they'd talk about if they did somehow meet. He would sound like a lunatic if he told her he had met her in his dreams, and even worse if he admitted that he was in love with her. They'd lock him up again, only this time it would be in the psychiatric ward.

KATHRYN PEPPERED her friend with questions all that afternoon and in the days to follow. Adele answered as many as she could and shook her head sadly at the rest.

Adele has no idea who Gavin is. The truth of it was finally sinking in. *Of course, if the program never took place,* Kathryn sighed, *then Gavin doesn't exist at all. The whole thing has been a figment of my imagination, a story to keep me going while I was in a coma.*

It was a reasonable answer—one Adele had suggested and the only one that made sense. She had agreed that it was Kathryn's way of telling herself she was ready to love again. The part that blew Kathryn's mind was how real it felt and how the "reality" could be so powerful that it blocked out the memories of what did happen.

According to Adele, she'd been on her way to meet with the dean of the university when the accident happened. She'd been T-boned by someone running a red light. Kathryn's family had pressed charges, and the driver, who had been drinking, was now doing time for his offense.

It seemed ironic that the woman he hit was someone attempting to rehabilitate prisoners. Kathryn wondered what she'd say to the man if he ever came to her for counseling. Ultimately she knew. The accident was her creation as much as it was his. It was a match to both their vibrations, and for that she could hold no malice.

She questioned what her family hoped to gain by taking the matter to court. *Probably reimbursement for the pain and suffering they've endured,* she mused sarcastically. It was typical of them, but she didn't want to dwell on it.

She thought again of the wonderful family she'd created for Gavin in her dream world. It made sense that she'd create them the exact opposite of her own self-serving, dysfunctional family. She hoped to meet people like the McDermotts one day—hoped too that they might have an amazing son like Gavin.

The nurse came in, interrupting her thoughts, and began to change her intravenous. They had removed all but one tube, and the doctor informed her she'd be free of it the following day. She would then begin physiotherapy. She'd broken bones in the accident: her leg, her ankle, and several of her ribs. They had healed, but spending nearly two months bedridden had taken its toll on her body, and she needed to regain her strength.

The woman was about to leave when she stopped, reached in the pocket of her smock, and pulled out some slips of paper. "Several people inquired about you today," she informed Kathryn. "Oh, and one of these is a few days old. Sylvia was on duty." The nurse rolled her eyes, indicating she didn't think much of the woman. "She put the paper in her pocket and forgot about it. I hope it wasn't important."

Kathryn thanked the nurse and then looked at the papers. They had the date printed on the top corner, and as she shuffled through, she noticed the one with an earlier date. As she looked at the message, however, the color left her face. The piece of paper contained two simple words: *Gavin called*.

THE VERDICT WAS IN, and Gavin was in shock from the news he had received. Just as he'd sat waiting for his verdict almost eighteen years earlier, Gavin waited again that morning for the parole board to make an important decision about the course of his life. They must have liked what they heard in the interview, because instead of telling him he was eligible for a day pass every couple of weeks, they saw fit to grant him full parole. Gavin wasn't sure how he responded. He might have mumbled a thank-you; he couldn't remember.

The spokesperson for the small group of men and women explained that given his exemplary behavior and the fact that he had a home to go to and a family that had shown support consistently over the years, they were releasing him to his family's care. It would be house arrest, in essence, and he would have to report to a parole officer every two weeks. He wasn't allowed to travel more than two hundred miles in any direction from his farm. He had a number of other restrictions as well, such as abstaining from alcohol and drugs, but Gavin understood the reason for their concern.

There were plenty of rules to abide by, but he didn't care. He was going home! His parents had been notified and were on their way to pick him up. His prison term was officially over. He had a couple of hours to gather up his stuff and say goodbye to the other men before he met with the warden one last time. He could sum up how he was feeling in a word. *Numb*. What was happening didn't seem real. Although, from what he'd learned about reality, that didn't surprise him.

Saying goodbye was difficult. Expressing emotion wasn't something prisoners did, but he could see it in the eyes of the men that he called his friends. It was hidden behind jokes and slaps on the back, but it was obvious they cared and obvious they believed they'd never see him again.

The warden had a few kind words to say. He'd been a fair man, and Gavin respected him. After that, as Gavin sat alone in the warden's outer office, he couldn't help but look back on his time at Swenton. As he did, a desire began to grow. He knew—had known for years—that he wanted to give back and make amends for the crime he'd committed. As he sat waiting, an idea began to take shape in his mind.

He would be coming back. He didn't know when or how, exactly, he simply knew he'd be back. He wanted to help others with what he'd been given. First, however, he would need to learn all he could about Kate's program, her unique teaching. Then he'd look into coming back as a volunteer to help the men at Swenton.

Maybe this is the reason for my dreams, he contemplated. *Maybe I've been selfish, thinking this is only about a relationship with Kate. I've learned so much, and now I'm in a position to share that information with others. I could be a mentor to the other men, encourage them and pass on what I've learned.*

My time here isn't over. It was a strange thought, yet one that gave him a sense of purpose and fulfillment as well as immense satisfaction. He was excited about his plan and eager to learn more about Kate's teaching. And he knew what he needed in order to begin.

KATHRYN HANDED the slip of paper to Adele as she walked in the hospital room the following day. Adele stared at the note, words forming silently on her lips.

After several seconds, she asked the obvious question. "Who is this?"

"Adele, I don't know of anyone else by that name," Kathryn declared. "Doesn't it seem strange that I wake up from weeks in a coma, having dreamed of someone named Gavin, and right away a person named Gavin calls? It's kind of freaking me out. I don't know what to do."

"Is this all there was to the message?"

"Yes, and there's another strange thing; look at the date on the message—it's the day I came out of the coma, but I just received it yesterday."

"Why would he only leave a first name? No last name or contact information? It's like he expected you to know him."

"I know," Kathryn shuddered. "It's really weird."

"Did you mention your dreams to anyone else, any of your family?"

"No, but I was thinking the same thing, that someone was just…playing a joke." She paused. "Please say it wasn't you." She knew deep down that her friend would never stoop to such a hurtful practical joke, but she needed to hear it.

"I would never do that!" Adele exclaimed.

"I'm sorry." Kathryn regretted her accusation. "I know that; I really do. I'm just trying to sort this out, examine every possibility, that's all."

"All right, then," Adele said, having moved on and already deep in thought. "Why don't we work backward in solving this? Let's assume that there *is* a man named Gavin—the very one you met in your dream. You had detailed information about him. You knew his file. He was at Swenton, right?"

"Yes, I see what you're saying!" Kathryn was excited to have some direction. "Let's find out if there is a Gavin McDermott at Swenton."

"Exactly."

"Adele..." Kathryn stopped to think through their plan of action. "What if there is? What do I do if there is actually a man named Gavin McDermott incarcerated at Swenton Prison?"

"Obviously you're not going to call him out of the blue and tell him you've been dreaming about him," Adele laughed.

"Or pay him a visit," Kathryn added, aware of how ludicrous it sounded.

"We're getting ahead of ourselves." Adele put the situation back in perspective. "Let's take one step at a time and trust that the next step will reveal itself. Who knows? We may still find a reasonable explanation."

Kathryn had tried to think through all the "reasonable" explanations. She had asked one of the nurses about the possibility of her getting the note by mistake. She was more than willing to believe that it was meant to go to someone else, someone who did have a friend or relative named Gavin. The nurse followed up on it; she even talked to the girl who had taken the message. It had been several days, but the girl remembered the conversation. She said the man had definitely inquired about Ms. Harding's condition and was hesitant to leave a message, but then changed his mind and told her to say that Gavin called.

"Will you call Swenton for me?"

"Why don't I try right now?" Adele looked at her watch. "It's going to drive you crazy until you know something. It's only four o'clock there. I might be able to get someone in administration."

"What are you going to say?" Kathryn was as nervous as she'd ever been. "They might not give out information on the prisoners."

"If not, then we'll find another route," Adele assured her.

Kathryn waited anxiously as Adele went down to the main lobby to use the phone. If someone by the name of Gavin McDermott was a prisoner at Swenton, she had no idea what she was going to do about it. If not, they were back to square one, wondering who had left the message.

The minutes seemed endless as Kathryn waited to hear what news, if any, her friend would return with. She searched Adele's face as she entered the room. Adele looked perplexed, and Kathryn knew she'd learned something. "What did you find out?" she demanded eagerly.

"There is a Gavin McDermott," Adele shook her head as if she didn't quite believe what she was about to say. "He's been at Swenton for the past seventeen and a half years. But…" she took a deep breath before she continued. "He's not there anymore; he was just released."

"Released?" Kathryn repeated. "Fully released already? Did they say if he's had any partial release, any day passes?"

"No, and they wouldn't give me a forwarding address or any particulars about his time at Swenton."

Kathryn's head was swirling with the new information, but just as quickly, she was making a plan. "Can you do more research for me? His parents' names are Carol and Richard. They've lived on a farm near Redding since Gavin was little. He has a sister named Sandra. I don't know her married name, but she's a nurse.

"There must be a way to get information on prisoners," Kathryn continued, barely stopping for a breath. "See what you can find. The incident took place in Redding. It was gang related. Check back to see what news stories you can find. It was nearly eighteen years ago; fall of 1992, I believe."

Adele was scribbling down information as fast as Kathryn spoke.

"He's thirty-five, maybe thirty-six by now. His middle name is…" Kathryn probed her memory, trying to recall information she'd read about him in his file. "I want to say Richard, after his father, but I don't think that's right. I think it's Edward. Try both names.

"He's well over six feet and weighs, I don't know, two hundred and twenty, maybe more. Much of it is muscle; he's in very good shape." Kathryn could see his body in her mind, and again she felt passion stir within her. Suddenly she wanted him to be real, wanted him to be the Gavin she'd come to know—the Gavin she'd fallen in love with.

It was a long shot, but she wanted to give it all she had. She wouldn't rest until she'd learned why he had been such a dominant player in her dreams for the past weeks, and why now it seemed he was trying to contact her.

Chapter 16

Gavin watched eighteen years of his life fade away as he exited the gates of Swenton Maximum Security Prison as a free man. He felt strangely calm now, but his parents were overcome with emotion at the suddenness of his release.

"You'll need some things," his mother declared, not even trying to hide the excitement in her voice.

"The basics, I guess," Gavin agreed. "I could definitely use some new clothes. No stripes, though," he laughed. It was a joke, of course. Prisoners at Swenton wore regular clothes, but they were prison issue with no style or individuality.

"There's something else I'd like to get," he added hesitantly, not wanting to take advantage of their kindness. "...if you don't mind."

"Whatever you need, Gavin, don't hesitate to ask," his father assured him. "It's no problem. Don't worry about money either."

"It's not the money." Gavin had saved most of the paltry wages he'd made in prison, and he was given a sum from the government upon release. Over all it wasn't a lot, but it would help him feel somewhat independent until he could find a job. "I mean, I want to pay for my own things. What I'd really like to get is a computer. Do you mind if we look around today?"

"Of course we can do that," his father replied. "Do you know what you want?"

"No, not really," Gavin shrugged. "But I'm sure we can find someone knowledgeable."

With those objectives, they went to one of the city's mammoth shopping malls. For his parents it was a labor of love, but for Gavin it was an adventure. Buying new clothes was enjoyable, but shopping in an electronics megastore was a dream come true; he had no idea the kinds of things that existed in such a place. He kept the sales clerk busy for much longer than most people took to buy an entire new home entertainment system. Gavin left the store that afternoon with a laptop computer and a wealth of knowledge that would be invaluable in the weeks to come.

KATHRYN RETURNED HOME recovered in body, stable in mind, but wavering significantly in spirit. Her life had been turned upside down. Her work at the university had been suspended while she was in the hospital, and now it looked as if it would be terminated. Her team had found other employment. Adele had gone back to private practice. It was as if everything she'd worked so hard for had crashed with her in the car that day.

Beginning again felt overwhelming. The rehabilitation program had been Kathryn's sole focus since her husband died. Now she didn't know where to turn or what direction to take, other than setting up her own practice again as Adele had done.

It had been years since she'd been in private practice. Working with people was what she loved, but it was her belief in the program she'd developed, her conviction that it could radically change lives and transform the nation's penal system, that had driven her, nearly consumed her. Now she wasn't sure she had what it would take to pick up the baton again.

On top of the confusion over what to do with her life, she had the knowledge that everything she'd had Adele verify about Gavin was true. The problem was, Kathryn had absolutely no idea what to do with the information.

Whenever she thought about the program, she thought of Gavin, and whenever she thought of Gavin, she grieved the loss of what could have been. Not so much for herself. It had been so much bigger than just a relationship. She realized that now. Ultimately, Gavin represented the success of her program. Without Gavin, there was no success, no program, and sadly, no hope.

She tried to pull herself together. She knew that the principles she wanted to share with prisoners to help transform their lives were the very things that could help her too.

It was easier, somehow, to see the sty in someone else's eye than to see the log in her own. Other's problems seemed apparent and the solutions clear-cut, while her own issues were muddied and confusing. Nevertheless, as the wisdom of the age-old book stated, she needed to take the log from her own eye before she could see clearly to help others.

Kathryn realized she not only wanted but needed the kind of counseling she offered others. It was an easy choice to turn to Adele. She made the appointment with her secretary, knowing Adele would be hesitant to see her in a professional manner. She'd been Adele's boss and had more years of experience in the field of psychology, but Adele was gifted. She understood and taught the same things Kathryn did, plus she knew what Kathryn had experienced while in a coma. Adele was the obvious person to help her sort things out.

"Kathryn, it's good to see you," Adele welcomed her friend into her office. "I have a two o'clock appointment, but if you don't mind waiting for a bit, I'll have Judith reschedule the rest of my patients. We can get some coffee or a bite to eat…"

"I am your two o'clock appointment," Kathryn interrupted her friend.

"You don't have to schedule an appointment with me, Kathryn. We can talk any time. Besides, I ought to be the one paying you for advice, not the other way around."

"I haven't been living what I teach," Kathryn admitted. "I've gotten off track. I'm confused, and I need someone to help me sort it all out. I wouldn't put myself in anyone else's hands. I need your help, and I think this is the best way to go about it."

"All right, if this is what you want."

"It's what I need."

GAVIN WAS HONORED that his sister joined their parents in welcoming him home. With her kids out of school for the summer, she'd taken a month off work, and Gavin was eager to spend time with his sister and his nieces. Sandra was two years older than he was. They hadn't exactly been close as teenagers, but as adults they had a connection.

He was glad for her expertise, which she claimed was minimal, when it came to using the computer. There was so much that Gavin didn't know, and he was hungry to learn.

She'd done a rather extensive search on Kate's teaching and excitedly shared what she'd found. "I'm impressed. This teaching is simple yet powerful. The rehabilitation program Ms. Harding is proposing to establish in prisons is remarkable. There's nothing like it out there. I've looked at some of the results of the work she and her husband have done, and it's really impressive. It's literally changing not only the mental health profession but the world of medicine as well."

Gavin was happy to hear his sister speak highly of Kate and her program. He knew her methods worked; he'd experienced it—albeit in an altered state of consciousness. Regardless of how it had come to him, he had definitely benefited from it.

He told Sandra about his dream of helping the men at Swenton, and she encouraged him. "I think that's a great idea, Gavin. You know what it's like in there; you know what they're going through. You could get this message across better than anyone. And not just Swenton. I mean you could start there, but you could eventually speak to other prisons as well. It would have been nice," she added, "if you could have met this woman and learned from her directly. It sounds like she had a real passion for this work."

Gavin winced inwardly as he listened to his sister's comment and longed to share what he knew. He hated being less than honest with his family, but he knew how absurd the truth sounded. "Maybe I will yet," he replied, "…one day."

KATHRYN FELT AT EASE in Adele's care. She took on the role of patient and was willing to listen to whatever her friend and counselor had to say.

"I'd like to touch on a couple of things," Adele began. "This might seem like an irrelevant issue, but would you object to being called Kate?"

The question left Kathryn completely taken aback. She'd not yet shared with Adele the conversation they'd had in her unconscious state, nor had she mentioned that Gavin called her Kate.

"I know you were Kate as a child," Adele said gently. "And I know your reasons for changing your name.

But I've always felt Kate suited you better. Kathryn feels...I don't know...contrived somehow. Like you're pretending to be someone you're not."

The words were the same as in the dream. Kathryn didn't know how to respond.

"It's not a big deal," Adele apologized. "I didn't mean to offend you. It's just...something I've thought of before, and it may be significant."

"Gavin called me Kate," Kathryn said softly as she dealt with the emotion that arose. "He could see the part of me I've been hiding. You're right, you know. In fact, we've had this conversation before."

"We have?"

"Well," Kathryn laughed, "technically I had the conversation with myself. Just now...the way you said that...it was almost exactly the way I dreamed it."

Adele's look of confusion lingered for a moment longer. Then she shook her head and laughed with her friend. "Wow, this is really going to be interesting. Tell me, did we have any other conversations I should know about?"

"Yeah, we did, but I'm not sure they're relevant right now. What was the other thing you wanted to discuss?"

"I was wondering what condition your inner space is in," Adele replied. "It's the basis of what we teach others, so I thought it would be a good place to begin."

Kathryn knew that Adele was right in bringing it up. She hadn't taken much time for herself, hadn't given much thought to her own spiritual condition. It was undoubtedly the reason she was feeling so low.

"It feels cluttered and disorganized right now," she admitted. "It's supposed to be a sanctuary, yet it feels like a place that's been ignored and uncared for, for too long."

"Well," Adele declared, "we really got to the heart of that one. It's kind of fun working together like this. I forgot how well we read each other."

Kathryn nodded. They did make a good team. She was truly grateful for her dear friend. Relaxing in her chair, she closed her eyes, already anticipating what would come next.

Adele led her through a guided meditation, and Kathryn was delighted by how good it felt to be guided rather than the one doing the guiding. It had been a long time since she'd reversed roles with anyone.

As she listened to Adele's voice, Kathryn soon began to feel renewed comfort in the familiar place she'd created long ago. She looked around her space with fondness and a longing to spend time there again. She felt safe once more as she connected to the part of her she'd been ignoring.

Soft, satin tears slipped down her cheeks as a warmth radiated through her. The rhythm of her breath comforted her, and she felt her vibration begin to rise. She was at home, and that felt tremendously refreshing after being away for so long.

When Adele finished speaking, Kathryn opened her eyes and wiped away the tears on her cheeks. "I needed that," she smiled. Her time was almost up, and she wanted to keep their meeting professional. "I've booked two more sessions this week. I believe we're on the right track." She took Adele's hand, squeezing it lovingly. "You really are very good."

"Thanks, Kath…" Adele paused and they looked at each other, both knowing the question on her mind.

"Call me Kate." For the first time she felt the name truly suited her. "I think I'm ready for a change."

GAVIN WAS TRULY enjoying time with his family. He and his dad spent afternoons in the shop working on projects. They shared the same work ethic, paying close attention to detail. They were both perfectionists who took pride in their work, and Gavin found it very satisfying. There was yard work and gardening to be done as well, and he gladly helped out.

He still couldn't express how it felt to be a free man. He was glad to have the understanding Kate had given him. He felt no resentment or bitterness when he reflected on his time in prison. It was the contrast he'd needed, and now it was behind him.

He spent hours on his computer and made interesting connections on the Internet. Talking to others who could relate to his situation was helpful; he'd already made friends with other ex-convicts. The people he met there were literally all over the world and all over the map when it came to their beliefs, their mental and emotional states. Some were bitter toward the prison establishment. Others were repentant and wanted, like Gavin, to give back in some way.

He found people interested in discussing spiritual things, and in the relative safety of a social networking site, Gavin felt comfortable sharing his paranormal experiences as well as the insight he'd gained.

He felt uncertain about going out in public, meeting new people or running into people he'd known before he went to prison. His parents encouraged him, telling him their neighbors and friends would accept him. He knew he'd have to integrate into society eventually, but he didn't feel ready.

At times like that, he missed Kate. She would have the right words to say. Thinking of her and researching her work on the Internet had brought her memory to the forefront of his mind. She frequented his thoughts and dreams now, and Gavin welcomed her. Still, he longed to reconnect with her physical counterpart.

Chapter 17

Kate knew what she had to do. The thought was so persistent she had to follow it. She'd resisted, wanting to make sure she was doing it for the right reasons, but now she felt confident that she was. Without hesitation, she called the representative for the constituency Swenton Maximum Security Prison was in and gave the woman a summary of her proposal. Fortunately, she'd heard of the rehabilitation program Kate had developed and was in favor of the idea. She'd even offered to set up a meeting with the prison administration staff. It was two days away, and Kate began preparing for the trip.

"I wish I was going with you," Adele acknowledged as she watched her friend pack the following evening.

"I do too. You don't know how much!"

"This is just a start," Adele assured her. "Once they see the results, they'll want to initiate the program in all the prisons across the nation."

"And once that happens," Kate insisted, "I want you with me."

"Wild horses couldn't keep me away."

Kate's decision meant offering her program despite the lack of funding—funding that would have ensured her a paycheck, allowed her to have assistants, not to mention covered expenses associated with such an endeavor. She was offering it to Swenton as a trial for one year, if they were interested. She had money saved up; she wouldn't suffer financially. She'd also received a sizable settlement from the accident, and given it had come to her largely because of her family's greed, she decided this would be the perfect way to use the ill-gotten money.

After saying goodbye to Adele at the airport, Kate left for the all-important meeting. Her nervousness existed on several levels. She wanted her program to be accepted and wanted to begin the work she'd been honing for so many years, but the fact that it was Swenton left her with jitters she couldn't seem to calm. She could see the facility clearly in her mind and wondered if it could truly be the way she'd imagined. It would be strange knowing it was where she'd met Gavin, knowing he was no longer there.

Kate arrived and found her hotel easily with the car she had rented. It was the same hotel she'd stayed in when her team first came to the city to begin the program. Everything about the hotel was familiar, yet in reality she'd never been to the hotel, or even the city before. It was rather disconcerting. She understood about the paranormal, having studied the topic and talked to people who'd experienced such things. But she'd never experienced them herself—until now. It was exciting, but it left her in unfamiliar territory.

The warden and two members of the board at Swenton, along with the government representative she'd spoken to, were present for the meeting. Kate began with the pitch she'd used many times over the years, this time modifying it to reflect that she was alone and willing to offer her program and her services voluntarily. The responses seemed favorable, but with the decision left to a vote, Kate had to wait—possibly for several days—to receive an answer.

The next day she familiarized herself with the city. *Re-familiarized* was a more accurate term, as she'd already been there in some capacity, and the experience was still fresh in her memory. She drove by the Denny's Restaurant that Gavin had pointed out and stopped at the same Starbucks they'd been to. As she did, she questioned how her experience with Gavin could have been merely an illusion, when her knowledge of the city was so real.

Does he know, too? she asked silently. *Somewhere, somehow, is he thinking of me, too? Was this a parallel reality we both encountered, or was it just a complex conjuring of my own imagination?*

She believed in the connectedness of all beings and in the possibility of things she didn't understand. Nevertheless, the situation made her feel somewhat unsure of herself. On top of all that, there was another phenomenon that even with her wealth of knowledge she couldn't begin to explain. A picture frame like the one Gavin's father had made for her was in the box of items retrieved from her car after the accident.

She hadn't said anything to Adele, hadn't known what to say. There was no picture, and the glass was broken, but it was evidence proving that what she'd experienced was in some way real.

Gavin's question about reality plagued her, now more than ever. She couldn't find an answer that satisfied her. *He could probably explain it better than I could,* she mused. *He seems to have an understanding, a deeper grasp of those types of things.*

She wished she could talk to him, but she knew she had to trust the Universe to work out the details. If they ever were to meet again, it wouldn't be by her meager efforts. She had to follow her intuition, stay connected, and find fulfillment in the moment. The grander schemes of life would take care of themselves. She truly believed that.

Kate waited patiently for the call from the prison administration and was pleasantly surprised to hear from them the next morning. They said they had a few more questions and wanted to meet with her again. She went expectantly, feeling confident their answer would be yes. She was met by smiling faces, and that helped boost her confidence even more. Their questions had to do with the administration of the program, the length and frequency of the sessions—all things that were flexible and rather insignificant in her mind. Overall, they were pleased to welcome her to Swenton and offered their complete cooperation with the program.

The warden called her aside as the others left his office. "Ms. Harding, may I have a word with you?"

"Yes, of course," she replied and invited him to call her Kate.

"I wanted to mention something that I thought might be of interest to you. There's a man, a former inmate actually, who's interested in volunteering at the prison. He's familiar with your teachings and is hoping to be able to mentor some of the men here.

"It's quite a coincidence." The warden scratched his head. "When he made the appointment to see me this morning, I had no idea what he wanted to discuss. Since you're both here, I wondered if you'd like to meet him. I didn't say anything to him yet; I wanted to ask you first."

A tightening sensation in her chest told Kate the man he was referring to was Gavin, and that knowing made it difficult to breathe, let alone answer the warden. She nodded and forced a smile. "I'd be happy to meet him."

She couldn't think of a satisfactory resolution to the situation. The thought of seeing Gavin unexpectedly left her nearly paralyzed with anxiety, but discovering it was someone else altogether would be hugely disappointing. She had no choice but to follow the warden as he led her to one of the outer offices where the man was waiting.

AS THE DOOR OPENED, Gavin stared at what he was sure must be an illusion. Entering ahead of the warden was the woman who had been in his dreams for months. Kate stood before him, alive, healthy, beautiful, and very real.

He couldn't take his eyes off her. He noticed she was staring, too, but realized it could very well be in response to the shocked look on his face. Averting his eyes, he waited as the warden made introductions. Then he shook her hand politely as he tried desperately to think of what to say.

After the warden left them alone, Gavin spoke. "Kate…" he shook his head, regretting his blunder. "I'm sorry…Ms. Harding. It's nice to meet you."

"No, please, call me Kate," she responded graciously.

He couldn't help notice the beseeching look in her eyes. "Kate," he stammered. "Your teaching…it's amazing. It's really…um… helped me a lot."

"How did you learn about my work?" she inquired, her eyes asking more than her words.

"I…" Gavin met her eyes and sent a silent message. *Please remember me, Kate.* "It's a long story," he said, exhaling audibly, "…and kind of a strange one."

"I've got time. Would you like to go for coffee?" She extended the invitation easily, but Gavin couldn't miss the look on her face: subtle apprehension mixed with a kind of longing, as though she was begging him to hear what she couldn't say aloud.

Gavin's inner knowing confirmed his suspicions. He didn't know how the conversation would unfold, but he knew without a doubt that she knew him. He eagerly accepted the offer of coffee.

"Do you like Starbucks?" she asked. "There's one not far from here."

"I don't know," he shrugged. "I've never been. I'm game to try, though." As he watched her, he noticed a slight frown followed by a strained smile.

"ALL RIGHT, let's go, then." As Kate led the way, she silently questioned Gavin's response. *If he's never been to Starbucks, then he hasn't experienced the same alternate reality that I have.*

She was dying to find out if he really did know her and if so, how, but she decided to be cautious. It had been a shock seeing him, and all kinds of emotions were erupting inside her; she didn't want to say something that could jeopardize any future relationship they might have, whether it be personal or merely work related.

Gavin seemed uncomfortable as they entered the coffee shop. She reminded herself that it hadn't been long since his release and that he was probably still discovering new things every day.

"What would you like to drink?" she inquired, watching him.

"Coffee, I guess." Frowning at the menu board, he laughed, "Do they even serve it here?"

"Do you trust me?" she asked, taking the term *déjà vu* to a whole new level. "Why don't I order the drinks and you get us a seat?"

"Sure," he shrugged. "Thanks."

Kate ordered what he'd already tried and liked in her dream, hoping for the best. As she waited for the barista to make their drinks, she was glad for a moment to collect her thoughts. She had no idea what Gavin was about to say or how she would respond. She could only hope it was what she'd been longing to hear. After several calming breaths, she reminded herself that it was all unfolding perfectly.

Drinks in hand, Kate headed to the table. Gavin smiled as she sat down. He took a sip of the latte she handed him. "I could get used to this," he remarked, looking pleased with his drink. "Things have really changed since..." He stopped mid-sentence and gazed at her intently. "Kate." He took a deep breath. "You asked me how I know about your work."

She nodded, wanting to assure him that she was open to hear what he had to say, confident that she already knew what it was.

"Something happened to me...while I was in prison. I had this dream...sort of..." He swallowed hard. "It might even have been...I don't know...some sort of...alternate reality."

He was struggling, and Kate longed to ease his discomfort by telling him everything, Still, she proceeded with caution. "I'm familiar with those kinds of things, Gavin," she replied, her heart pounding. "I've experienced them, too."

"You have?"

She wondered why it surprised him that she could relate to what he was saying, but waited for him to continue. He described his time in the infirmary and the dream he had of her being at Swenton, teaching him. She listened intently, and when he stopped, she waited, expecting him to continue, but he didn't.

"So what happened then?" she asked, trying to be casual, but nearly bursting with suspense.

"After I got out of the infirmary, I found that none of it had actually happened. But I still had all that I learned from you...and the memories."

Kate caught something in the way he'd said *memories*. There was more he wasn't saying, but she didn't know how to ask. She felt disappointed. It was obvious that his experience differed from hers—or that she had just continued hers, embellishing it with the fantasy of a relationship, ending it with a kiss.

"In our sessions together, we talked a bit about reality. I didn't understand it at the time, but I've thought about it since. It seems to be multidimensional with layers that people can experience consciously or unconsciously. I think a lot of it is probably unconscious," he added, looking at her with questions in his eyes.

"That's remarkable, Gavin. I've been searching for a definition for reality, a way to sum up what I've been experiencing. You just described it perfectly."

Gavin didn't respond; he stared into his drink while unspoken words echoed between them. There was so much Kate wanted to share, but she was tentative, fearing she'd say too much.

"You said you can relate." He looked at her with conviction on his face, a determination to say what needed to be said. "But...have you just experienced the same kinds of things..." he paused. "Or did you experience what I did...*with* me?"

He'd gone the extra step. Kate was incredibly grateful for his willingness to be vulnerable. Now it was her turn. "Yes, Gavin, I did. I mean...I think it was the same," she clarified, hoping to find a reason for the discrepancies in their stories. "I was at Swenton; I experienced the sessions just as you described. You were making great progress...but..."

"What is it?" Gavin begged. "What happened?"

She was afraid but willing to be vulnerable, too. She knew she could tell him more, maybe not all, but definitely more. "I was there with my colleagues," she began. "We set up the program and spent weeks meeting with the men in groups and individual sessions. I was amazed at how quickly you were learning and understanding what I taught. I was so impressed by your progress that I recommended you for early parole, and they approved you for day passes..." she paused. "But that's where I get confused. Our stories seem to differ."

"What do you mean?"

"You were approved, Gavin, and I accompanied you home. It was a Thursday. We left at eight in the morning and stopped here at Starbucks on the way to your parents' farm." She could see the surprised look on his face, but continued. "I met your parents...and your sister and her husband and their two little girls. Your mom made brunch, all your favorite foods. You showed me around the farm. It was lovely. Your family was wonderful. You seemed so happy..." She was shaking now, almost uncontrollably.

Gavin touched her arm in a comforting gesture. "What happened, Kate?"

Kate closed her eyes, summoning the strength to continue. As difficult as it was, she had no choice. "I sprained my ankle. You helped me to the house. Sandra examined it to make sure that it wasn't broken. We had a bite to eat and then left to go back to the city." She summed up the facts, but omitted the most relevant details.

"Is that all?" he asked gently.

"No," she admitted, nearing tears. She'd been forced to reduce the experience to a dream, but as she retold it now, it was as vivid as the day it happened. She wasn't sure she could tell Gavin the rest without breaking down. All of a sudden she felt self-conscious sitting in the middle of a busy coffee shop. "Do you mind if we go somewhere else?" she asked. "I'm staying at the Rideau; it's not far from here. Maybe we could find a quieter place to talk."

Kate and Gavin stood up together and walked silently to their cars. Arriving at the hotel minutes later, they entered the lobby, and Kate looked around. Several sofa groupings were set back from the main reception area, and she led the way to one. It was a much better spot, more conducive to the type of conversation she perceived they were about to have.

Gavin was quiet, obviously waiting for her to continue. He sat facing her on one end of the sofa, his arm draped over the back. He looked great. She'd hardly noticed his appearance earlier; she'd been in too much shock. He wore dress pants with a shirt and tie, and his hair was trimmed. He looked older, more mature, than Kate remembered.

She took a deep breath and found the courage to tell the rest of her story. "You fell asleep on the drive home. You'd mentioned that you hadn't slept the night before, so I knew you must be exhausted. You didn't look comfortable, though, and I tried to adjust the seat back without waking you. I took my eyes off the road for a second…"

It was apparent by the look on his face that Gavin hadn't experienced anything close to what she described. Yet the revelation hadn't upset him; he was listening intently, waiting for her to conclude.

"I heard a car horn. I swerved in time to miss the other vehicle, but I lost control and we rolled. When everything settled, I looked at you, and you had blood all over your face and chest. I tried to find my cell phone…" Her voice was shaking again, and she took a moment to calm herself.

"You kept telling me that everything was okay, but it wasn't. I was afraid you were dying and it was all my fault. And then you told me…"

She couldn't do it. She couldn't repeat the words Gavin had spoken to her; it was too much. *If he didn't have the same experience, then he never said the words and maybe never felt them either.* Kate longed to go back and unsay what she'd already spoken. She could envision a giant chasm between them now, and she didn't know how to bridge it.

Gavin leaned toward her and took her hand. He looked her in the eye and finished her sentence. "I told you I loved you."

She gasped. "How did you know?"

"I may not remember that particular incident," he said softly. "But it's what I've been feeling and what I've been wanting to say ever since I met you."

"But how...?" She looked at him helplessly. "I really don't understand any of this."

"I don't either," he admitted. "But we can't deny it, and we can't undo it. Maybe together we can try to figure it out."

She nodded her head, liking the way he said *together*. It felt good, yet she still had resistance. Her mind was sifting through all that had taken place.

"What did you say?" he asked, grinning.

She frowned, not understanding his question.

"What did you say," he asked again, "when I told you I loved you?"

"I told you that I loved you, too," she sighed, feeling such enormous relief at having shared her story that she decided to include the final important detail and have everything on the table. "And then I kissed you."

"I'm sorry I wasn't there for that," he teased, caressing her hand with his thumb.

"You're here now," she looked at him longingly, throwing caution aside, wanting more than anything else in that moment to be in his arms. Suddenly her desire manifest, and Gavin's arms were around her, holding her tight. She was crying, although they were tears of joy, and he comforted her for a moment before he looked into her eyes and then silently at her lips. He wiped away a tear that had rolled down her cheek and met her lips with a kiss that far surpassed any she had previously dreamed of.

The moment was magical, and she gave herself to it completely. She had fallen in love with Gavin Mc-Dermott and thought she'd lost him forever. Now he'd returned more wonderful than she'd imagined, proving their love was not bound by time or space. It was a mighty force that defied all reason, offering hope when none was visible and a glimpse of the future that seemed to have been lovingly written for them by All that Is.

Chapter 18

In Gavin's first waking moments, he questioned if what he'd experienced with Kate had been a dream. The day they'd spent together had been surreal. Seeing her at the prison, going out with her, learning that she'd felt what he had and experienced even more—it left him reeling. He couldn't wait to see her again.

They'd planned to meet that morning. So much needed to be discussed. Kate had come to set up her program at the prison, and Gavin knew he was meant to be a part of it. It felt right. But there was more now. They had a history together, a mysterious love that bound them. It was hard to understand but impossible to deny, and Gavin wanted nothing more than to embrace it and allow it to unfold.

The kiss they'd shared was extraordinary, as if all the kisses in his dreams had culminated in that moment and combined to create the perfect kiss. Now he wanted more; he wanted all of her. But he was content to wait. As much as he felt Kate's love and passion, he felt her hesitancy too. She was afraid of moving ahead too quickly.

He told his parents about the meeting and shared his excitement about the possibility of working with Kate. He would have to tell them about the budding relationship soon, too, but the timing wasn't right. They wouldn't understand all that had taken place in a realm he couldn't explain. Even so, he knew the situation would work itself out. Kate had already met his parents, sort of, and she loved them. He was confident that they would love her, too.

He arrived at her hotel by 11:30 and they went for lunch. She looked young, carefree, and even more beautiful than the Kate of his dreams. He couldn't take his eyes off her. She wore form-fitting jeans and a colorful sleeveless top that showed off her figure beautifully in layers of gauzy fabric over a solid tank top. She had a slim build and was above average height for a woman. Dressed in trendy, casual clothes, she looked sexy and ten years younger than the image she'd first portrayed in his dream.

They went in his car. It had been his next major purchase after the computer, and he couldn't describe the liberating feeling of being behind the wheel again. It was another expression of freedom that he thoroughly enjoyed—one that most take for granted, but one he could now enjoy on a level that went beyond the ordinary.

"You look really good," he smiled as he glanced over at her. "I like this look on you."

"I haven't spent much time on my appearance in the last few years," she admitted. "I threw myself into my work after my…" she paused, and Gavin wondered if she was ready to discuss her late husband. "After Kevin died."

"Yesterday, after we were together, I went to my hotel room, and when I looked in the mirror I realized something. I felt young, but I looked much older. I don't know how that happened. So I decided to do something about it. I found a salon and got my hair cut and then went shopping. It was fun."

Gavin was touched by the lengths she'd gone to update her style for him. He'd seen her beauty right from the beginning; it was an integral part of who she was. Now he found her not just attractive but sexy and irresistible too. He reached for her hand and held it as he drove.

They arrived at the restaurant and found a place to park. Before opening his door, he turned toward her and for a moment gazed at her. He wanted to let her know how he felt but didn't want to be too intense; they still needed to talk about where their relationship was headed. He wanted to tell her how beautiful she was without it sounding like he was just coming on to her.

Before he could decide on the right words, she reached out and tenderly stroked his face. Smiling, she kissed him lightly on the lips and then turned to open her door. From any other woman it might have been a tease, but from Kate it was a clear message telling him where she was emotionally. He still needed to take it slow.

Gavin worked at keeping the conversation light as they ate lunch. There was so much they didn't know about each other, and he enjoyed learning new things about Kate.

She was athletic. He'd judged from her tall, trim figure that she would be well suited to sports, and he wasn't surprised to learn that she enjoyed tennis and racquetball and was an avid swimmer. She'd competed in swimming competitions in college and had made it to the national finals one year. When her hunger for knowledge and growing desire to help people through the field of psychology won out over her love of sports, she'd given her heart and dedicated her life to pursuing that dream.

Kate was animated as she spoke, using her hands to accentuate what she was describing. Gavin liked that about her. She was talkative but drew him into the conversation with questions. She frequently tucked her now-shoulder-length hair behind her neck. A fringe of hair cascaded down across her forehead and blended flawlessly into the rest of her golden-brown locks, and she brushed it aside occasionally as she spoke. Gavin imagined running his hands through the soft-flowing mane. He had in his dreams, and he longed to experience it again. He continued to daydream, not aware that she had stopped talking.

"You're not saying much; is everything okay?"

"I'm sorry," he replied, deciding to be frank with her. "It's just that we're here together. It's hard to believe. I've had to pinch myself a few times already. You're everything that I dreamed of. Not to mention, you look amazing. I can't take my eyes off you."

"I know we should talk about what's happening between us..." She looked down, and Gavin sensed that her hesitation about engaging in a relationship may have escalated. "But I don't know where to start. It's so far beyond anything I've ever known. Part of me wants to let go and trust that it will take us somewhere wonderful; another part is cautioning me to be careful and take it slow.

"If this was an ordinary relationship," she continued, "I'd be concerned about our age difference. I'd question the fact that you've just spent nearly eighteen years in prison, and I just happen to be the first woman you've met. Other than our paranormal experiences, we know very little about each other; we may not have much in common."

Gavin was quiet. He hadn't looked at the situation from her perspective, but he could understand now why Kate was reluctant to move forward too quickly. He wanted to address her concerns and quell her fears, if possible, but had to acknowledge the truth in what she'd said. He decided to try anyway.

"Kate," he reached through the maze of items on the table and took her hand. "Those are valid concerns. I'm certainly not experienced in matters like this, but it seems to me that every couple must face issues that could potentially make or break the relationship if they let them."

She remained silent, so he continued. "What we have is bigger than that. It's a connection that goes beyond what we know and understand. Something greater than us is orchestrating this. We're like pawns in a giant game of chess."

"Maybe that's the part that scares me," Kate admitted. "I've always felt in control of my life, at least somewhat, and this feels out of control. Not in a bad way," she quickly added. "It's just that I've always trusted what I know to guide me."

"You said that one part of you wants to trust, and the other is being cautious. Which one feels better?" he asked, knowing it was the kind of advice she'd given him in the past.

She looked up at him, frowning, then smiled and shook her head. "You're right. I have a perfectly good guidance system, and I'm disregarding it, trying to think rationally."

As Gavin watched her take a deep breath, he prayed that she would find the strength she needed to allow her heart to guide her.

"In the car," she began quietly, "when I thought you were dying, I didn't want to live without you. When I woke from the coma, you were the first person I asked for. Even when I learned that everything I thought had happened, didn't, I couldn't stop thinking about you. And I came here…" She was on the verge of tears again, and Gavin longed to hold her. "Not just to implement my program at Swenton. I came with the hope that somehow I'd find you."

"We found each other, Kate," he smiled, his heart swelling at her revelation. "It just feels right. I don't care about the difference in our ages. I'm glad you're the first woman that I laid eyes on after so many years behind bars. And I think we do have a lot in common. I want to work with you in the prison. I want to learn all I can and help the men just like you do. I want to spend time with you and get to know everything about you—even if it takes a lifetime. I like racquetball and swimming. I'll learn how to play tennis, and if you say you like ballroom dancing, I'll learn that too. I love you, Kate."

KATE COULDN'T HOLD BACK the flood of tears. Gavin was the most extraordinary man she had ever met, and he was unashamedly declaring his love for her. Suddenly she couldn't remember why she'd doubted her feelings for him. She was in love with him—truly, deeply, and completely. Not only that, but she had renewed faith in the greater part of her that always guided her perfectly. Now she wanted to let Gavin know how much she loved him. She wanted to give herself to him completely. Wiping away her tears, she smiled, "Let's get out of here."

As they entered the hotel lobby, she saw him glance at the sofa they'd occupied the previous day. She took him by the hand, leading the way to the elevator. He looked at her, a question in his eyes.

"I love you, Gavin," she responded. "I know that now, and I'm ready to move forward in our relationship. I'm ready to let it be all that it can be."

When the elevator doors closed, he took her in his arms and kissed her with an intensity that left her breathless. She responded in kind, and suddenly the passion that he'd been suppressing and she'd been denying was released. It was the most powerful feeling she'd ever known. They were two people deeply in love, and they'd both been deprived of the physical act for too long; they could hardly wait for the privacy of a hotel room.

Once inside, however, Gavin stopped kissing her and looked into her eyes. "This means more to me than just sex," he whispered, his breath labored from the urgency of their kisses. "I want this to be amazing for both of us."

Kate had no doubt that would be the case, but his regard for her was touching. She began unbuttoning his shirt with one hand, while the other explored the hard muscles of his chest and arms. Removing his shirt, Kate took a moment to look at Gavin's impressive upper body, now fully exposed. It was breathtaking and perfect, a replica of the gods, and it made her ache for all that he had to offer.

She led him to the bed and lay down, her eyes beseeching him to join her. There they continued undressing each other and exploring the treasures beneath the layers, their passion mounting to new heights until it erupted in the most beautiful of all human acts.

Afterward, Kate lay back exhausted but completely satisfied. Although Gavin was somewhat inexperienced, he was a gentle and considerate lover. She hoped that their first time together had been all he had anticipated.

Not wanting to ask him directly, she looked at him and saw the answer written on his face. He turned to her, smiling broadly, and she had to laugh. The look of wonder and amazement on his face was priceless.

All of a sudden a thought occurred to her. "Gavin, was this...?" She hadn't entertained the idea that it might be his first time with any woman, not just her, and she wondered if talking about it might be uncomfortable. She tried to think of a less awkward way to phrase her question but found none. Instead, she propped herself up on one elbow and smiled back at him. "That was incredible."

Gavin nodded in response but remained quiet for a moment, looking pensive. "I started dating a girl in my senior year," he explained in answer to her unfinished question. "I was shy; I wanted to ask her out for months before I finally worked up the nerve.

"We did stuff," he asserted awkwardly. "You know what it's like when you're a teenager. Things can get out of control in the back seat of the car, but we never went all the way. She was too worried about getting pregnant. It was never...like this."

He was blushing, and Kate realized she'd never found him more attractive.

"This is the first time that…"

She didn't let him finish. She kissed him again, reigniting the passion they had barely begun to discover. The layers they had yet to explore were deeper than just physical, but for the moment that was all they could think of. They were embarking together on a journey of joy and pleasure beyond anything that either of them had known, and every new discovery was an epic adventure to be emblazoned forever on the pages of their hearts and minds.

Chapter 19

Kate lay in Gavin's arms, listening to the rhythm of his heart, feeling happier than she had in a long, long time. An afternoon of lovemaking had left them both spent, and Gavin had fallen asleep. She was content to stay there forever. She'd found bliss and didn't want to do anything that might take away from it. Even the basic necessities could wait.

The past two days had taken her from the fleeting dream of a soul mate to the loving arms of a man who was more than her wildest dreams could have conjured. She could hardly believe it. Gavin was a gift from the heavens, yet he was her own creation, a manifestation that had come in response to her vibration, and she to him in the same fashion.

It was a remarkable system—one with no room for error. A person couldn't receive anything they weren't a perfect vibrational match to. It was their thoughts, deliberate or otherwise, that determined their vibration, their point of attraction. Kate marveled at the perfection of it.

Gavin stirred and opened his eyes, a smile still evident on his face. Kate was sure the smile hadn't completely vanished all afternoon, and she was thrilled to be the source of his pleasure and the reason for his joy.

"I must have dozed off," he yawned.

"I thought we could order in...if you're hungry," Kate offered. "It's after six."

"We were going to go over the program. I guess we got kind of...sidetracked."

"A little," she smiled, thinking of how delicious their lovemaking had been. "I'm not meeting with the warden till Thursday, so I thought maybe we could look at it tomorrow. You know..." Her mind was easily drawn to the specifics of her program. "I think you could have a greater influence with this teaching than I could. The men will be able to relate to you, and once they hear what the program's done for you..."

"I love how passionate you are about your work," he interrupted. "It's what I first noticed about you. You weren't just selling something; you really believe in it."

"It's because I know that people are more than they believe themselves to be," she explained. "I think that everyone, even so-called criminals, can learn to see themselves in a new way. Maybe that's why I love the prospect of working in the prison system," she paused, realizing again her motivation for the particular work she'd chosen. "There's more room for movement, more opportunity for growth, and more reward in seeing lives changed in an environment like that."

"I was thinking of something earlier," Gavin inserted. "You've worked with several of the men already, just like you worked with me. You know their situations, their specific needs, as well as their response to your teaching."

"You're right!" Kate exclaimed. "I can't believe I didn't think of that. I was so focused on the experience I had with you, I totally overlooked the fact that I know those men's files already. I spent just as much time with them. You know them, too," she added excitedly. "Maybe together we could tailor the program to suit their needs right from the start."

They ordered room service and began talking about the other nine men that had been in Kate's group. Gavin was able to provide additional information, affirming details that Kate had suspected but had no evidence to support.

"Your contribution to the group sessions will be invaluable," Kate informed him. "The men are going to be skeptical at first, reluctant to share, possibly even rude and disruptive. Having you with me is going to make a big difference."

"I'm excited to see what effect this program can have on others," he agreed. "But...how do I explain knowing all this? I mean...I've only been out for a matter of weeks, yet I've been learning this and applying it for months now."

"We'll have to come up with an answer for that one, and probably a few other questions, too," she replied as the bizarre reality of their unique situation impressed itself on her again.

Gavin seemed to read her thoughts. He moved toward her and she leaned into his embrace. "How can we be sure this is real?" she asked, not really expecting an answer.

"It might not be," he smiled, holding her close as if she might somehow vanish. "It depends on what definition of *real* you use. I've been thinking about that too. If anything is real, love is. If that's the case, then I know what we have is real, and it can endure anything. It may be the only thing we can count on in this crazy experience called life."

Gavin's wisdom astonished her as it had more than once in her dreams. Adele had suggested that he was connected to a higher knowing, and Kate wanted to learn more about his journey. "Gavin, what do you do to maintain the spiritual connection that you have?"

"What do you mean?"

"Do you meditate or pray...I mean, is this something that you had a conscious desire to learn about, or has it come to you naturally?"

"Before I met you, I used to spend half the night dreaming—although I was awake," he clarified. "It was more like daydreaming, my way of escaping. When your sessions started, I realized that your guided meditations weren't all that much different. Only you took me further than I'd ever gone before." They both realized the double meaning in what he had just said and began laughing.

"My pleasure," Kate said, thinking of their unforgettable first time.

"Mine too." He kissed her hair.

"Did you feel a connection," she asked, returning to the topic, "when you meditated?"

"It was addictive, even when I did it on my own. It was the only time I felt free, and I couldn't wait to return to it every night. After I met you, the meditations changed and you became part of them. You were always in my dreams, guiding me." He smiled at her. "We had amazing adventures.

"Then one night," he continued, "I was feeling confused, questioning what was happening to me, and I started talking to you...in my mind. I asked you questions and you answered me. After that, I talked to you all the time and learned things from you in my dreams."

"Is that how you knew what I would be talking about in my sessions? You freaked me out sometimes, bringing something up right before I was about to introduce it."

"I don't know. The sessions I experienced were different." He was quiet for a moment and then asked the question that was on both their minds. "Do you think we'll ever figure this out?"

Kate wasn't sure. She'd certainly attempted to sort it out in the past two days. They'd had similar encounters. They'd been a part of each other's reality, but the differences seemed to indicate that the realities were unique, separate even, yet connected in a way she couldn't understand. Still, she had to trust her Higher Self. "I believe wisdom comes to us when we ask," she replied. "We'll understand this one day."

"So when I asked for wisdom in my dreams, was it coming from you, or did you represent something bigger, some Greater Knowing we're all connected to?"

Kate stared at him in awe. "Gavin, that's it!" she exclaimed. Her inner knowing validated what Gavin had just said, but the understanding was lacking. She sought clarity as she put her thoughts into words. "Maybe that's what all this represents. We are to each other that greater part of ourselves. It's the connectedness of all beings epitomized in this unique relationship we've created."

"Wait. You told me that once. I asked who you were, and you told me you represent all that I am and all that I want to be."

"What else did I say?" Kate laughed. "I want to know what other impressive wisdom I'm spewing as a representative of All that Is."

Gavin thought for a moment. "You told me that you're everywhere I am; you're always with me. You said that my dreams are your dreams, and that my experiences are yours, too. You said that we're inseparable….and you explained the reason I chose to go to prison," he added.

Kate knew the reason. He'd shared it with her on their drive to his parents' farm—the drive he had no memory of. If he'd told her at the time that he had learned it from her in a dream, she wasn't sure she would have believed him.

Their lives, their thoughts, their dreams, and their realities had somehow become intertwined. Gavin was such a part of her life and she his that there was no clear line where one left off and the other began. It was a lot to understand and accept.

Kate could feel the truth of it, but she had questions. *If we represent the greater part of each other, it makes sense that our realities would intersect. But why now and never before? Why have I never heard or read of anyone who has experienced similar things? And was our time together just a dream, or was it real?*

Gavin had described reality as multidimensional with layers that people can experience consciously or unconsciously. Hindsight had given them a clearer understanding, but in the midst of such an extraordinary experience, it seemed impossible to know what was real and what wasn't.

Who's to say this isn't just another dream? Kate had to dismiss the thought. It didn't feel good; it wasn't serving her. She chose instead to focus on what Gavin had said earlier: Love is real; it may be the only thing that is. And love, she possessed. She had been assured of Gavin's love, and no matter what happened in the future, she had to trust that nothing could take that away from her.

GAVIN LEFT KATE reluctantly that evening, still awed by what had transpired. He kept telling himself that they had their whole lives ahead of them, but it was hard to be patient when all he wanted was to be with her every second.

He'd invited her to his parents' farm the next day, and she'd readily accepted. In light of that, he decided to prepare his parents for Kate's arrival. Inviting the director of the rehabilitation program he was involved with to meet his parents after knowing her only two days might seem a bit sudden. Not only that, but his mom was intuitive; she may very well sense that something was going on between them.

Carol was in the living room, curled up on the sofa, reading, as he walked in. He sat down on the recliner facing her. "How was your day?" she asked.

He would have liked to tell his mom everything. He felt guilty hiding anything from her, especially something so exciting. "It was great," he responded, trying to apply just the right amount of enthusiasm. "Mom, Kate and I need to go over the program tomorrow, so I invited her here. I hope that's okay."

She looked at him with a slight crease in her brow, but responded politely. "Of course, that's fine, dear."

He could tell that she already suspected something, and he wasn't sure what to say. To fill the awkward silence that followed, he began telling her about Kate's background and the work she was doing.

"Gavin," she interrupted, looking tentative. "Do you have feelings for Kate?"

"Mmm." He nodded affirmatively.

"Does she know?"

He nodded again, knowing he couldn't end the conversation there. "Mom," he began uneasily, "there's something I haven't told you."

Carol looked at him with surprise and curiosity but remained silent.

"When I was in the infirmary this spring, I had this dream. Only, it was more than just a dream. I met Kate somehow, and I learned from her.

"When I got out and found that none of it had actually happened, I was tempted to write the whole thing off as a weird hallucination or something. But when I started looking into it, I found that she did exist, and she taught the very things that I'd discovered. So I decided to learn all I could. I even hoped to meet her one day, but I never dreamed it would turn out like this.

"I had no idea that she'd be at the prison the other day when I went in to talk to the warden. When she found out that I was familiar with her work and wanted to help out, she invited me to go for coffee. That's when she told me that she'd had a similar experience. She dreamed about me, too, Mom," Gavin paused, looking at his mother for acceptance, "...when she was in a coma.

"Something's happening between us," he concluded, trying to make his incredible story sound normal. "It's something we don't really understand, but we both feel it."

His mom remained silent, and Gavin was curious to know what she was thinking. It wasn't the whole truth, but he felt it was as far as he could go and as much as his mom would be able to accept. Now looking at her face he hoped he hadn't said too much. "I know that sounds strange…"

She shook her head. "What's strange is that I've had a feeling about this. I had a dream awhile back about you and a woman you'd met. It's funny...you brought her home here, and as soon as we met her we knew—both your father and I—we just knew she was right for you."

Gavin was elated, but he had to ask, "So you don't think it's odd? The dreams we've had and how we feel about each other...so soon?"

"God works in mysterious ways," Carol smiled. "It's best not to question it. You know how you feel. You can trust that to guide you."

Gavin went to bed that night feeling as though his life was being perfectly orchestrated. It filled him with a bubbling sense of euphoria and an invincibility, the like he'd never known. He could be or do or have anything. Although he didn't have lofty dreams and ambitions, those that he did have were unfolding perfectly. It caused him to think about what else he wanted in life.

He wanted someone to spend his life with, and he was pretty sure he wanted to have children one day. He could see himself married to Kate, but he didn't know how she felt about children. The fact that she didn't have any at her age led him to conclude she'd either chosen not to or wasn't able to. Gavin knew he loved Kate enough to let go of that dream. He had two nieces he adored, and Sandy had confided in him that she and her husband were trying to get pregnant again, so he would have the experience of a baby in his life.

He tried to turn his attention to other areas of his life and imagine what he would create if he were truly unlimited, but instead fell asleep with thoughts of Kate, memories of their amazing afternoon, and anticipation about the day ahead.

Chapter 20

Driving to Gavin's farm was like replaying the scene from her dream. Kate sipped her favorite latte and turned the radio to an 80s channel, but she didn't need the props to help her relive the day. She passed fields and buildings that she had seen before. When she got to Redding, she remembered the turnoff as if she traveled the road frequently. The final stretch to Gavin's farm reminded her of the issues he was wrestling with as they neared his home.

More than anything, she was thrilled to be seeing Gavin again. She might have been nervous about meeting his parents, but Gavin had called the night before and told her of his mom's reaction. Afterward they'd talked long into the night, and she felt like a young girl in love for the first time.

As she pulled into the McDermotts' yard, a dog bounded up to the car, barking and wagging his tail in greeting. She questioned the variance from her dream visit and immediately wondered what other differences she'd find. Gavin came out to meet her and settled the dog, which he informed her was a recent addition to their family. "I'm imagining that I'm kissing you right now," he winked.

"We'll have to behave ourselves," Kate replied, unable to keep the smile off her face. "I don't want your parents to think I'm some cougar trying to snatch herself a delicious morsel."

"That's quite the analogy," Gavin laughed. "I kind of like it."

He led the way into the house and made introductions. Kate was pleased to recognize Gavin's parents and relieved to feel the same warmth she'd received during their first meeting. After a few moments of small talk, Gavin's dad excused himself to work in the garden, and Carol joined them as they moved into the living room.

"Gavin's told us about your program," Carol smiled at Kate. "It sounds impressive. I think it's great that he's going to be involved in it, too."

"It is," Kate agreed. "I worked hard trying to get the funding for a trial program. I wanted my team here with me, but now that it's just me, I'm grateful to have help. Gavin's ideal for this. He can relate to what the men are going through. He's already helped me see things differently. We're going to adjust the program slightly, now that he's given me insights on the men I'll be working with."

"Tell me more about the work you do with the men." Carol sounded genuinely interested.

Kate was thrilled to talk about her work. It was truly her passion. She gave Carol a summary of the program. "Our first goal is to help the men find their emotional/spiritual center. I call it their inner space. Through guided meditation, I help them create and maintain their space. It's the foundation they need to begin the rest of the work.

"This space becomes their control room, so to speak, the center, the hub. I help them see that the condition of their space determines the condition of their life. It's based on the premise that our thoughts determine our experience; what we think about expands to become our reality.

"Once they begin to see the correlation between their thoughts and what plays out in their life, I help them see that individual thoughts and even entire belief systems can be changed thereby changing the outcome of their experience."

"That sounds marvelous," Carol exclaimed. "Gavin mentioned that you've already had success with this teaching in other areas. It'll be great to see what you can do to help the men in Swenton."

"I can't guarantee success, but I can offer hope, and I can provide tools for those willing to change. Most people who've committed a crime have done so from a place of extreme powerlessness. Often the act is a way of trying to take back power in their lives. I show them other ways of reclaiming their power.

"I also introduce them to the idea that all human beings are interconnected and part of something much bigger. Whether they believe in God or want nothing to do with the idea of a higher power, this process works and can be tailored to meet their individual needs."

Kate noticed Gavin watching her as she spoke, and saw love radiating from him. She was illuminated when she finished, as she often was when she shared her teaching. His mom was smiling, too.

"Well," Carol stood up, "that all sounds so interesting. But I'm sure you have work to do to prepare for this, so I'll leave you two alone. I have peas in the garden that need picking. Kate, you'll stay for supper?"

It was more of an assumption than an invitation, but Kate smiled graciously. "I'd love to. Thank you, Mrs. McDermott."

"Oh please, call me Carol."

Kate thought she noticed her wink at Gavin as she turned to leave the room. She nearly laughed, but managed to hold it until Carol had gone outside.

"Did I see right?" she asked, still trying to suppress her laughter. "Did she wink at you?"

"Yeah," Gavin moved toward her on the sofa. "She knows something is going on between us, and she obviously approves; she's a very perceptive woman. I think we should confirm her suspicions."

"I agree." Kate leaned into his kiss and was catapulted into rapturous bliss. Kissing Gavin was the most intoxicating experience and the only thing she wanted to be doing in that moment.

The blissful moment didn't last nearly long enough, however, as their kiss was interrupted by the side door banging. They quickly created a distance between them as a little girl, whom Kate recognized as Gavin's niece, scooted into the living room and stopped short, obviously not expecting to see a strange woman sitting beside her favorite uncle. When Gavin opened his arms, the little girl giggled and ran happily into them.

Kate watched the heartwarming exchange and felt the usual longing that accompanied such a scene, but this time a new thought entered her mind. *Gavin's great with kids; it's so obvious. Will a future with me be fair to him if it means no possibility of children?*

Carol came in minutes later and apologized for the interruption. "I forgot to tell you that Rob was dropping off the girls today. Sandy's working days, and he has a meeting this afternoon. We'll try to keep them entertained outside."

Gavin kissed the little girl and sent her off with her grandma before turning back to Kate. "Now, where were we?"

Kate sighed. She hated to spoil their precious time alone, but needed to address the subject, and the moment seemed opportune.

"What's wrong?"

"There's still so much we haven't talked about. When I see you with your niece...I mean...you're a natural with children, Gavin. I'm sure you'll want kids of your own...one day."

The look on his face told her she was right, and she felt her stomach tighten.

"Kate," he took a deep breath and reached for her hands. "My life hasn't exactly been normal, but I don't regret it. I don't know how the rest of my life will unfold, but I have to trust it will be what it's meant to be, that my desires will be met somehow. Right now my greatest desire is to be with you. I don't just mean for now; I want to spend my life with you. I want to marry you, Kate."

The impromptu proposal shocked Kate. She wasn't sure if it was a proposal or just an impulsive statement, an indication of his desire in the moment.

"Gavin, I'm forty-two…" She stopped, not sure how to finish the sentence.

"And I'm thirty-six," he responded with passion evident in his voice. "I've spent nearly eighteen years in prison for murder. As much as I love kids, I'm not sure it's a good idea to have them under those circumstances. How do you explain to a child that his father killed someone?"

Kate hadn't thought of it from that perspective but could understand his concern.

"I'm so sorry, Gavin. I've only been thinking of myself. We'll work this out."

"While we're on the subject," his voice softened, "I was wondering…why didn't you have kids? I mean… were you not able to or was it a choice?"

"Both, really. I always thought I would one day, but Kevin and I were so caught up in our work. The year before he died, I started thinking more about it. You know, the biological clock ticking and all that. I stopped using contraceptives, but nothing happened. Now I'm not sure I can conceive."

"But you still would," he looked at her optimistically, "…if you could?"

She sighed. To be honest, if she was suddenly presented with the opportunity to have children, she was quite sure she would take it. But there was so much more to consider now. She looked at Gavin, trying to read his thoughts.

"I think so," she admitted.

"Then marry me." He took her hands again. "And let's let whatever happens, happen. If we're meant to have kids, we will. We'll find a way to explain all this to them. Who knows," he paused to smile, and Kate loved him more in that moment than she ever thought possible. "Maybe there's a little soul waiting up there —someone who just happens to want an ex-con for a father and a wise, mature, accomplished woman for a mother."

She had to laugh at his delightful picture. When he talked, things made so much sense. When she was with him, all potential problems faded away, and the future became a bright, well-groomed path waiting for them to walk down together. She wanted more than anything to take that path. Her heart was already there calling her forward, urging her on.

He looked in her eyes, waiting for her response. Still, she hesitated. Her rational mind wanted to have its say. *How can I agree to marry someone I've known only two days?* she argued.

Taking the other side of the debate, she countered, *Well, that's not really true; I've known him so much longer than that. But what will people say?*

Since when have I cared what other people say? I need to do what's right for me. Can I trust my heart, though? Can it really be that simple?

She knew the answer to her questions, and she knew the answer she wanted to give Gavin. Every fiber of her being was screaming *Yes!*—quickly drowning out the weak objections that common sense had tried to bring up. She looked at him and smiled.

"Well…?"

"Well, what?" she teased, wanting to hear his proposal again.

"Kathryn Harding…" Still holding her hands, he went down on one knee beside the sofa. "Will you marry me?"

"Yes," she said faintly, then repeated it, leaving no doubt in either her mind or his. "Yes!"

He gazed at her for a moment, love shining in his eyes, a mixture of joy and relief on his face. Moving to the sofa beside her, he picked her up effortlessly, cradling her in his powerful arms. Kate threw her arms around his neck and kissed him. She'd made her decision, and she knew without a doubt it was the right one. The rapture she felt in the moment was proof that she was indeed following her path to joy.

Chapter 21

Gavin was living a dream. He had just proposed to the most fabulous woman in the universe, and she'd accepted. Details needed to be discussed, of course, and decisions made—such as whether to tell his family right away—but he quickly dismissed the thoughts and focused on kissing the woman he loved, caring only about the moment and how good it felt.

"I can't believe all that's happened in such a short time, but it feels right," he shook his head, astonished and overjoyed, as he set Kate down on the sofa.

"I know," she smiled dreamily. "And that means it *is* right." She gazed at him lovingly and asked, "Do you want to tell your parents right away, or should we wait a respectable amount of time before we announce we're engaged?"

"What's respectable?" he laughed. "An hour, a week, a month?"

"I'm not sure," she grinned. "But they'll know something's up just by the look on our faces. We should probably try to concentrate on work. We can go over the files I started on the men nearing their parole dates."

"You're probably right; we should," he agreed. "But I'll really have to concentrate. With you here beside me, agreeing to be my wife, all I can think of is how much I want to make love to you."

"Me, too." Kate stroked Gavin's face.

Gavin knew his mom would be in soon to make lunch, and as much as he wanted to hold Kate and kiss her endlessly, he knew he had the self-control to wait. They would create more opportune moments, but for now, the work they'd planned to do together was important, too. He moved a reasonable distance from her on the sofa and smiled, "Let's get to work."

By the time Carol returned, they'd discussed more than half the men that had been in Kate's sessions. Her organizational skills were impressive and the questions she asked, thorough. Gavin couldn't answer them all, but the information he did provide excited Kate. He admired the enthusiasm she had for her work.

Carol prepared a lunch of fresh produce from the garden, delicious potato salad, and cold chicken. Gavin had a healthy appetite, and his mom seemed to get immense joy from pleasing him with her culinary skills.

Gavin tried to keep lighthearted conversation going at the table. It wasn't difficult with Sandra's girls present. They loved to be the center of attention as all kids do, and he enjoyed asking questions and teasing them. He had come to know the girls well in the short time he'd been home, and he loved them both dearly. The oldest seemed so grown up for her age and liked to engage him in various topics of conversation. The little one was able to pull his heartstrings with a smile or a blink of her eyes, and he was powerless to resist.

He tried not to look at Kate, but when he did, he couldn't hide the smile that wanted to light up his face. He realized it was a mistake to sit across from her; it was hard not to gaze at her the whole time. He decided to change the seating arrangement for their supper meal and have her beside him. Then all he'd have to resist was the urge to touch her or play footsies under the table.

When the meal ended, Gavin was quite sure they had succeeded in hiding the news that in truth he was dying to share with his parents. He was confident that they would not only approve but give their blessing. However, he had to think of Kate, too, and decided that letting the idea of marriage settle for a few days would probably be best.

Kate offered to help Carol clean up the dishes while Gavin played with his nieces on the living-room floor. Now that he and Kate had discussed having children, he couldn't stop thinking about it. He knew he shouldn't get attached to the idea because she'd mentioned her concern about not being able to get pregnant. But he let his mind go there anyway. He liked the idea of a son, but he loved the reality of the little girls that were climbing on him; he knew he'd be thrilled to have a daughter.

The women came into the living room, where Carol informed Gavin that Kate was a lovely girl. She thanked him for bringing her out to meet them and then announced that she and his father were taking the girls into town to see a matinee. The exuberant look on his face must have been telling. His mom gave him a look that conveyed her approval of Kate as well as her delight in offering the young couple time alone.

After his parents left and Gavin was certain they were several miles down the road, he picked Kate up off her feet and held her in a loving embrace. He smiled as she wrapped her long legs around him, her full, billowy skirt not hindering her movement in the least. "You must have been thinking about this as much as I was," he said, noting her eagerness as she unbuttoned his jeans.

"Maybe," she teased. "Or else I'm getting really good at reading your mind."

With their desire escalating quickly, they moved together down the hall and into the spare bedroom. The door barely closed before Kate's passion reached a gratifying height and she moaned in pleasure. It was intoxicating to move inside her and feel her body respond to the sensations that were engulfing her. He was nearing a climax himself, but wanted to take her to even greater heights. Together, in the moments ensuing, they found a new definition for ecstasy. For him it was Kate in his arms, a part of his body, a piece of his soul—creating together the most heavenly experience known to man.

"Oh God!" Kate cried, laboring for breath.

Gavin was feeling the same but couldn't speak; the glorious sensations were holding his body in rapture. Finally he leaned against the door, breathing heavily, and opened his eyes to look at the woman in his arms. "I love you so much," he murmured.

She responded, eyes bright with tears and a look that spoke volumes. They collapsed onto the bed and held each other for a while longer, silently savoring the intimacy, not needing words to communicate the fullness of their hearts. He hadn't known it was possible to be such a part of another person that the lines of separation nearly vanished. He was truly happier in that moment than he had ever been, or had ever expected to be.

The most exciting part was knowing they were just beginning their journey, at least this stretch of it. He was sure that they'd journeyed before, many lifetimes, many adventures—all as wonderful as the one they were embarking on.

IT TOOK DELIBERATE effort on both their parts to return to the work they needed to do that afternoon, but Kate's enthusiasm soon reemerged. The information that Gavin provided and the way the modifications to the program unfolded soon rivaled her excitement about her future with Gavin.

Gavin's parents returned home with the kids, and Sandra arrived shortly afterward. Gavin made the introductions, but for Kate it was a repeat. Sandra seemed excited about the work Kate was doing and began asking questions that Kate was more than happy to answer.

"I've read quite a bit about your program and the philosophy behind it. It sounds remarkable. It seems to me that the men must come from varying backgrounds and environments, and they've all had different experiences. How do you deal with the kinds of issues that must come up and still stay on track with the program?"

It was an intelligent question and one for which Kate was well prepared, having dealt with many critics over the years. She could sense, however, that Sandra's question came from a place of pure interest.

"Well," Kate began. "Research shows that the factors shaping our lives, the paths we take, and the decisions we make are not primarily the result of the outer environment we're exposed to, but rather the inner environment, the connection between our head and our heart, our mind and our soul.

"Two people can be exposed to the same physical environments—even share the same DNA, in the case of identical twins—yet turn out to be radically different. Therefore we don't see the past as highly relevant in a person's life. How they feel in the present moment is the primary issue we address. The past can appear to have significant ramifications on the present, but our goal is to help them break free from that limiting mind set. We do it by dealing with their inner space.

"Once change happens on the inside, that person is never the same again." Kate glanced at Gavin and saw that he was smiling. "That kind of permanent change can't happen through simply controlling a person's outer environment, which is evidenced by the prison system in our country. I'm not an activist," she clarified. "I don't get into the politics behind it; I just see the prison system as a place to start, with people who are, in most cases, more ready and willing to hear this than the average person."

Sandra, obviously enthralled by the subject matter, appeared to be hanging on Kate's every word. "That's amazing. It makes so much sense, too. We've seen evidence of that in Gavin." She smiled lovingly at her brother. "Keeping him in prison all these years was pointless because he found that inner change you're talking about. He became a different person. We could see dramatic changes in him, even if the officials couldn't."

"Many do find that connection on their own." Kate couldn't keep from looking at Gavin and sending him loving thoughts. "These men often come to their lowest point and cry out to whatever they perceive to be God or Source. Our work is to support or enhance that connection and give the men tools so they can continue to move forward, find confidence and identity, and ultimately reclaim their power."

"How do you do that?" Sandra asked, fascinated. "It sounds like something we could all benefit from knowing."

"There are plenty of ways to do it, but we've found specific tools that seem to work better than others. Of course, it depends on the person, but offering a variety of self-help methods allows each person to choose those that are right for them. Meditation is one that we've found to be invaluable in discovering and maintaining that inner connection. Teaching the men to view their emotions in a healthy way is important, too. There are so many screwed up ideas out there."

"Like the way boys are taught that crying is wrong?" Sandra offered.

"That's definitely one," Kate agreed. "Or the idea that anger is wrong and needs to be suppressed. We teach people to use anger as a bridge, a way to take back power and move to a better feeling place. I also lead them through a process called the 'Power Transfer,' where the person can feel the shift physically as power moves from the source of negative emotion to the inner space they've created."

"This is going to change so many lives, Kate," Carol interjected. She had been in the kitchen but was listening in on the conversation.

"It already has," Gavin added, beaming at Kate.

"How does the Power Transfer work?" Sandra asked. "That sounds really interesting."

"Why don't I demonstrate?"

When Sandra nodded her willingness to participate, Kate instructed, "Close your eyes and think of a topic that evokes negative emotion whenever you dwell on it." She knew the issue she wanted to address, but gave Sandra a moment to come up with something before she offered, "I felt negative energy when you talked about the prison system and the time Gavin spent there. Would you like to deal with that?"

"Wow," Sandra looked at her in surprise. "You picked up on that? You're good." She closed her eyes again, allowing Kate to continue.

"Tell me a bit more about how you see the situation and how it makes you feel."

As Sandra began to elaborate, strong negative emotion surfaced. Kate started the procedure using a mental image to help Sandra understand that the emotion was nothing more than a powerful blockage to the well-being she could otherwise experience in that area. Once Sandra was able to visualize the negative emotion and feel the power it held, Kate's words helped her imagine it returning to her body like a powerful wave. The process usually only took a few minutes, but in Kate's considerable experience, it nearly always produced impressive results. This time was no exception.

"Thank you!" Sandra bubbled with appreciation. "I had no idea I'd been holding on to that…or that it was affecting me in that way."

Kate had another technique she used regularly in her sessions. It was called "Moving up the Emotional Scale.$_3$" By deliberately choosing different thoughts, her students could easily move from negative emotion, which left them feeling powerless, to more positive, power-filled emotion. Although not as stimulating as the Power Transfer, over time this process produced lasting results.

"Now, when you think about the time Gavin spent in prison, do you feel different?"

"Yeah," Sandra nodded. "I don't feel as angry."

"From there, I would guide you into even better-feeling emotions. It often takes a few sessions, but the goal is to be able to think of any topic and find better feeling thoughts. For example, you may still feel frustrated or discontented with the idea. That's normal," she added. "But from there you could reach for thoughts of contentment or even optimism."

"Maybe," Gavin offered. "You could think of the time I spent in Swenton as a learning opportunity, the time I needed to gain the perspective I have now. Instead of wasted years of my life, you could see it as productive."

"Is that the way you see it?" Sandra asked, tears glistening in her eyes.

"Yeah," he smiled. "I do. I've learned to view my time there as valuable, and appreciate it. It feels so much better than the resentment I held on to for years."

Sandy began to cry, and Gavin gave his sister a hug. Kate watched the interaction, touched by the closeness they shared. This was the family she had met in her dreams. They were every bit as wonderful, and she was thrilled knowing she'd be a part of it.

Carol joined them in the living room, squeezing her son's shoulder as he hugged his sister. Her face shone with love and pride, and her eyes brimmed with tears. After a moment, she cleared her throat and announced that supper was ready.

Kate was surprised when Gavin took her hand and led her to the table. He pulled out a chair and once she was seated, sat down beside her.

Sandra didn't move from her spot; she stared at them, mouth open, obviously having had no idea that anything not work related was going on between them. Before she could speak, Gavin put his arm around Kate and asked a rhetorical question for his whole family to hear. "Can you see why I've fallen in love with her?"

Joining them, Sandra began to laugh, although her wide eyes indicated she still hadn't digested the news. "You're in love? When did this happen?"

Kate looked at Gavin to see if he would answer and noticed him hesitate. It was a tough question—one that Kate wasn't sure how to respond to either. She was willing to take a stab at it, but Gavin clasped her hand, answering his sister.

"We're not sure exactly," he laughed uneasily and glanced at Kate for moral support. She gave his hand a squeeze under the table and sent him a silent message of love and encouragement.

After Gavin had given his sister a condensed version of the story, Sandra responded with unbridled enthusiasm, addressing them both. "I'm so happy for you!" Turning to Kate, she added, "I don't think Gavin could have found a more remarkable person. I'm so glad you found each other."

News of their engagement could wait. They'd set the stage for it and no longer had to hide their feelings. For that, Kate was extremely grateful, not to mention relieved. She was bubbling over with emotion—emotion that was so far off the end of any scale she'd ever known, proving what she'd read and believed but never experienced, that even joy has no limit.

She thanked Sandra for her loving words and then thanked Gavin's parents for their kindness. "I never thought I'd fall in love again...after my husband died," she confessed. "But I can't deny how I feel about Gavin. I've never met anyone like him. He's wonderful."

"We think so, too," Carol beamed.

The rest of the meal was filled with laughter and questions, both about their relationship and about the program she and Gavin were planning to implement at Swenton. Kate happily answered, occasionally bowing to Gavin as he responded, even to questions about their work. She was thrilled that he'd become knowledgeable on a subject so dear to her heart, and that he already had a clear vision for the project they were about to undertake.

The evening unfolded exactly as Kate had imagined. The McDermotts were a close family, embracing newcomers as their own. It was late when Kate finally decided to pull herself away from possibly the most fun she'd had in years, if not ever. Sandra and her girls had already left, and Kate was enjoying a discussion with Gavin's dad. He was quiet in the group, but one on one, Kate discovered him to be intelligent and full of insight. He was open minded, too, and Kate could readily see that Gavin had received some of his personality from his father.

Gavin emerged from the kitchen. "It's a beautiful evening," he smiled at Kate. "Would you like to go for a walk?"

She couldn't refuse; the thought of it was irresistible. Outside, Gavin took her hand and they walked silently for a few minutes, the dog following at their heels. It was easy to enjoy the quiet, peaceful country setting. Having always lived in a big city, it was a decadent treat for the senses. Kate had never seen such a magnificent view of the heavens. As they moved away from the lights of the house, the sky came alive. The stars seemed to dance, and the constellations that enveloped them looked like a milky haze curving gracefully across the sky, put there by an artist's brush.

Familiar with the surroundings, Gavin led the way through the darkness and brought them to a bench just below the garden. A warm summer breeze carried delightful fragrances both from the garden and the creek below. Kate wanted the moment to last forever as Gavin put his arm around her and held her close.

"Mom said to tell you that you're welcome to stay…" he whispered, as if the sound of his voice might take away from the magic around them.

The invitation came as a complete surprise; she hadn't given thought to staying overnight. She had a meeting in the morning with administration staff at the prison, although it wasn't until ten o'clock.

"I'd been thinking about it," he continued, "but I know we didn't plan for it, and besides, I wasn't sure my parents would be comfortable with the idea."

"Are you sure she wasn't offering me the spare bedroom?" Kate asked cautiously.

"No, I made sure we were on the same page."

"What did you do, tell her you want to have sex with me?" Kate laughed.

"Not in so many words, but she got the idea. She's pretty cool."

Kate could tell that Gavin was smiling, and she snuggled closer.

"In some ways I think she still sees me as her little boy. Other times I can share my thoughts and feelings like she's a close friend rather than a mother. I don't know how I'd have made it through the past eighteen years if it hadn't been for her."

"Your family's incredible, Gavin." Kate looked up at the man she loved, the outline of his face slightly visible in the moonless sky. "I thought a family like that only existed in books and movies. Now I'm looking forward to becoming a part of it."

"You already are." He found her lips in the dark.

His words more than just moved her; they helped her realize that she was a part of his world. By becoming intertwined in Gavin's life, she had inadvertently created a fabulous family for herself, too.

"Do you feel comfortable staying?" he asked softly. She could hear the desire in his voice.

"I think so," she replied. "I mean, I want to. I'd love to stay with you. I just don't want to make your parents uneasy. This has all happened so suddenly that we barely understand it; I can't imagine how it must seem to them."

"You're not still worried about that cougar scenario, are you?" He ran his fingers through her hair. "I'm sure they'd never look at it that way."

They spent more tantalizing moments under the sparkling canopy before going back inside. Gavin's parents had gone to bed, leaving a trail of lights so they could find their way to the basement. In Gavin's room, Carol had placed a robe and slippers, clean towels, and a selection of toiletries. Her thoughtfulness was appreciated and so was the silent message letting Kate know that staying in her son's room was acceptable.

It was heaven to crawl into bed beside Gavin and know that their time together wouldn't have to end soon. As Kate relaxed on the soft mattress, she felt a fluid motion as she rolled toward Gavin. "A waterbed?" she laughed.

"I know," he responded, sounding embarrassed. "The whole room needs a makeover. You probably noticed the Van Halen poster on the wall, too; I've been meaning to take that down. My bedroom stayed in the eighties while the rest of the world advanced into the twenty-first century.

"Mom insisted on ordering a new bed. It should be here next week. I tried to tell them not to go to too much effort or expense," he explained. "I don't know how long I'll be here. It's kind of weird living at home with my parents when I'm thirty-six."

"You don't have to stay here, do you?" She was suddenly curious about the conditions of his parole.

"I talked to my parole officer about it. He's a really nice guy, by the way. He said the conditions are somewhat flexible. He figures that if I was to get work in the city, I could get a place there."

"Maybe now we can get a place together," Kate suggested. "Swenton offered me a year to set up the trial program and the possibility of two more years if all goes well. I was going to start looking for a place before I go… I have to go back home," she explained, "to take care of some things and pack up my stuff. I might be gone a few days."

"I'm missing you already," Gavin sighed, pulling her close. "But I love the idea of getting a place together. We can always fix up this room and spend some weekends here too."

"I'd like that," Kate replied honestly. She was watching their future unfold just like the bright, well-groomed path she had envisioned before. She realized too that had Gavin not shown up at the prison that day, she would be living and working on her own in a strange city, far from her friends. Now, with Gavin a part of her life, everything was magical and intriguing—an exciting adventure beckoning her forward.

Part 4
~Adele~

This time-space reality that everyone is perceiving is
nothing more than vibrational interpretation.

—ABRAHAM-HICKS

Chapter 22

The phone rang, waking Gavin from a deep sleep. He wasn't expecting a call so he let it ring, assuming his mom was upstairs and would pick up. By the fourth ring, Gavin had to conclude that his mom was in the garden. He reluctantly answered the phone, not really in the mood to make small talk with a friend of his parents or inform another over-zealous telemarketer that they didn't need their carpets cleaned. What he heard instead was his name and a woman's voice he didn't recognize.

"Hello...Gavin?" the woman asked. "Is this Gavin McDermott?"

"Yes."

She introduced herself as Adele Burgess and after a long pause, blurted out, "Gavin, I'm a friend of Kathryn Harding. I know this is a long shot, but I was wondering...is that name familiar to you? Do you know her at all?"

"I…um…" Gavin stammered, seriously questioning if he was still dreaming. He quickly stood up, feeling the coolness of the tiles under his bare feet. He looked in the mirror, rubbed his eyes, and ran his free hand through his hair—all in an attempt to assure himself he was sufficiently awake before asking, "I'm sorry, what name did you say? I don't think I heard you correctly."

"Kathryn Harding. She's a psychologist. Do you know of her?"

"Um…yes…" he answered tentatively, still not sure he was awake. "I've…heard of her. Why?"

Adele went on to inform him that Kathryn had been in a serious car accident and was now in a coma. She seemed reluctant to tell him more over the phone, and Gavin could hear desperation in her voice.

How on earth could she possibly know that I have any connection to Kate? The question screamed to be asked, yet Gavin remained silent as Adele told him she'd like to meet with him in person. He vaguely remembered agreeing to meet with the strange woman; he was still trying to digest the things she'd said.

Kate's in a coma. The news had come as a shock, but the fact that her friend was willing to travel across the country to meet him left him reeling. She was flying in later that day and asked if he could meet her. The hours dragged and questions continued to mount in his head as he waited to learn what the woman had to say.

Maybe Kate's been dreaming of me, too, Gavin speculated. The thought uplifted him for a moment, and then more questions emerged. *But if she's been unconscious, how would her friend know anything about her dreams? Is the woman psychic?* It was a definite possibility, but it fell far short of explaining the incredibly odd circumstance he found himself in. He twisted it around in his mind a while longer, trying to make sense of it, but it was no use; the situation was too bizarre. All he could do was trust that it would lead him somewhere and that the host of questions would soon be answered.

That evening, as he stood in the airport waiting for her to arrive, his apprehension accelerated. The absurdity of the situation hit him, and he began to have serious qualms about how their meeting would unfold. He'd been mystified, wanting to know how Adele had found him, but what he suddenly realized was that now he'd have to explain his unorthodox relationship with Kate, and he didn't know where to begin.

Gavin had yet to tell anyone about his supernatural experience in the prison infirmary or his ongoing dreams about Kate. He felt guilty sometimes, but what he'd experienced was so far beyond what he could understand, let alone explain, he wasn't sure how to bring up the subject. And if he did, he wasn't sure how his family would receive it.

He'd been home almost three months. At the beginning he'd tried for the sake of sanity to wipe the memory from his mind, but he'd been unsuccessful. Kate was as real to him now as she had been when he'd first met her in his dreams. She was his teacher and guide, and often his lover, and sometimes he could feel her presence—like the time his sister had taken him to Starbucks. It was soon after his release and his first time ever in the now-popular coffeehouse, but he'd had an overwhelming feeling that he'd been there before, and that feeling was linked to Kate.

He'd tried to determine what she represented to him and why she had been in the past and was still such a significant part of his thoughts and dreams. He couldn't help but wonder if they were of a paranormal nature, if he was actually connecting with her in an alternate reality. There was no other way of explaining how he could dream about something he knew nothing of, a woman he'd never heard of—but one that, he'd discovered since, did exist and taught the very things he now knew.

Once he had a computer of his own, unrestricted use of the Internet, and the freedom to use his time in whatever way he chose, he was shocked to discover the truth. He learned a great deal about Kathryn Harding, the woman he knew as Kate. He found a picture of her and read that her work, along with her husband's, was renowned. He continued to study and learn all he could because the subject fascinated him and because his hunger to learn and grow in those areas was strong. But it was more than that. The woman had some kind of spell over him and he didn't understand why.

She had been more to him than a nonphysical teacher. He was grateful for the teaching; it had helped him immensely. She'd drawn him to a place he'd never been before and shown him a part of himself he never knew existed. Moreover, she'd so indelibly impressed herself on him that he couldn't look at another woman without comparing her to Kate. She'd set the bar high, and he didn't want to—couldn't really—lower it.

He'd been dreaming of her when Adele called that morning. But unlike recent dreams, the encounter had been incredibly vivid and the details crystal clear. She'd been at his home and met his family. Not only that, but it seemed perfectly natural that they were planning their future together. His family had been more than accepting of their relationship; they were extremely happy for them.

Gavin put his thoughts on hold as people began flooding through the sliding glass doors that had just opened. He searched intently for a woman matching the description Adele had given, at the same time trying to calm his rapidly increasing jitters. By the time he found her in the crowd, she had already noticed him and was walking his way. As he watched the petite woman approaching, he assessed her and found himself relaxing a degree or two. He noted her pleasant appearance and professional demeanor. *She doesn't look like a nutcase.* He took a deep breath, still feeling uneasy, and found an element of comfort in the hope that he would soon understand why his dream world had collided headlong with reality.

ADELE NOTICED HIM immediately. He was a large man and stood out not only because of his size but because he was incredibly handsome and well built. In the seconds it took to walk across the airport meeting area, she noted that he looked nothing like she'd expected. His face had a gentleness to it, a look that conveyed quiet compassion and affability. The smile that he offered as she neared added to his approachability, and she felt her anxiety diminish.

"Gavin?" She extended her hand and he received it. He nodded in acknowledgment, but the look on his face, now that she stood in front of him, told her that his curiosity over her rather abrupt intrusion into his life was beginning to outweigh his natural inclination toward courteousness.

"I'm sorry I wasn't able to give you more information over the phone," she said, addressing his obvious concerns. "Could we go somewhere to talk?"

"Sure," he replied. "Do you have luggage?"

"Just this." Adele patted her shoulder bag.

"Let me take that for you," he offered politely.

As he led the way to the parking garage, she followed, silently rehearsing as she had on the plane. She'd known after talking with him on the phone that he would be able to help her, that Gavin was the man she was looking for. It was more than just a feeling; it was his silence in response to her revelation that had convinced her. Anyone else would have dismissed her as a lunatic. Furthermore, she suspected from his willingness to meet that Gavin had something to share as well.

In the car she took a deep breath and began her narrative. "I've known Kathryn for years. We've worked together, but she's also one of my dearest friends. Four months ago, she was in a car accident—a very serious one," she emphasized, trying to relay the facts without becoming too emotional.

"She's on life support, Gavin," Adele submitted gravely, "and her family wants to take her off."

He shot her a quick glance and looked away, but it was enough to see the pain in his eyes. She knew beyond a doubt that her suspicions were correct. Not only did he know Kathryn, he was intimately connected to her somehow. Adele was eager to learn more and hopefully fill in details of the mystery that had unfolded in the past few days.

"Why me?" he asked simply, rightly wanting to learn what she knew of him and how.

"A week ago, one of the nurses asked if I knew anyone named Gavin," Adele explained. "Apparently Kate said your name. I was excited when they told me she spoke; I was sure it meant she was going to be all right. Unfortunately, the doctor wasn't as optimistic. He said it's not uncommon for someone in a coma to utter a word or two."

They arrived at a coffee shop and ordered drinks before they sat down. Gavin was quiet, apparently taking in all that Adele said but offering nothing. She hoped he'd be more forthcoming after she shared all she'd come to say.

"Of course I had no idea who Gavin was. I'd never heard her mention the name before. I was curious, but it wasn't enough to go on.

"After the accident," she continued, "I was at the hospital every day. Her family hadn't arrived yet so the nurse gave me a box of Kathryn's things to take home —items retrieved from her car." Adele knew that what she was about to say would sound absurd, not to mention impossible. She decided that showing was better than telling, so she reached in her bag and pulled out a picture to show Gavin.

THE COLOR DRAINED from Gavin's face as he looked at the photograph that Adele handed him. It was a picture of him with his family, taken at the prison. "But how did she…?" he could find no further words to sum up the mind-boggling thoughts taking shape in his brain.

"I don't know how or why she had this picture with her things, but it helped me find you. Look at the inscription on the back."

He turned it over and had he not been sitting might have fallen over from shock. Words in his mother's handwriting said, "Thank you, Kate, for all your help and support in Gavin's life." She had signed it, "The McDermotts."

"I didn't find it until this week," Adele explained. "I got a sudden urge to look through the box of Kathryn's things I had at my apartment. The picture was loose in the box, and something's been spilled on it, but I could make out the Swenton stamp on your shirt pocket."

Gavin was speechless. He listened helplessly as Adele continued.

"That's when I called the prison to inquire about you, and they told me you'd been released." She looked at him, and Gavin saw tears form in eyes begging for his help. "I thought…I hoped…that maybe you could tell me more."

Gavin knew it was his turn to speak. It would be easier now after the incredible things he'd just heard and seen; his own story didn't sound so outrageous at all. After sharing what he'd experienced, both in the infirmary and since, he shook his head. "I don't really understand what's been happening between us. It's obviously a lot more than I'd suspected. All I know is that we're connected somehow, and it's more powerful than anything I've ever known."

He was almost certain now that he and Kate had been rendezvousing in a parallel reality. His dreams —most of them, anyway—were beginning to make sense. In recent weeks, he'd had the occasional dream that left him confused. Instead of learning from Kate or spending pleasant moments with her, he could feel the distance between them. She seemed far away, beckoning to him or calling his name. It pained him, but he couldn't understand it.

As he shared the seemingly unrelated dreams with Adele, he suddenly knew what they meant. "She's been asking for my help!" he exclaimed. "How can I help her? What can I do?"

"I wish I had the answers," Adele sighed. "I don't. But after hearing this, I'm even more convinced she's been sending us both messages."

"I'd like to see her."

"I was hoping you would. Maybe hearing your voice, feeling your presence, would bring her back."

"What about her family?" Gavin found it hard to believe they'd consider removing life support without trying everything that could be done.

"I begged them to wait a few more weeks before doing anything. They weren't close. Kathryn hasn't had much contact with them over the years, but unfortunately they're her next of kin, and they have the right to make the all-important decision whether she continues to live." Adele was crying now, and Gavin put his hand on her shoulder to try to comfort her.

After she'd composed herself, she added, "The thing is, the doctor told them that even if she were to come out of the coma, there's a seventy-five percent chance she'd have permanent brain damage. I think that's why they want to move on this. They don't want the responsibility of caring for her long term. "But I can feel it, Gavin. I just know she's okay, and she's asking for our help."

Gavin wanted nothing more than to leave that minute to go to Kate. He felt strongly, as Adele did, that he could make the difference. He'd sit and hold her hand, talk to her—whatever it took to connect with her and try to bring her back. But it wasn't that easy. A number of restrictions applied to his parole, and traveling that distance was one of them.

He told her his concerns, but she wasn't daunted. "I haven't followed the lead all this way to be stinted now. This has to work out. Somehow, we have to get you there."

Chapter 23

Adele had some ideas about how she might get the restrictions temporarily lifted on Gavin's parole, and she left him that afternoon with a promise that she would do all she could to arrange it. She'd been impressed by him, and now she contemplated again how the connection between Gavin and Kathryn, or Kate as he called her, had not only begun, but had become so powerful. Adele believed in the significance of past lives and the unity and connectedness of all beings, but she had never seen or had any firsthand knowledge of anything like what she was witnessing between her best friend and this man.

Although Gavin hadn't said so in words, Adele could sense the depth of feelings that he had for Kathryn. And she obviously felt a powerful bond with him, to be calling to him from another realm.

What is she experiencing now? Adele wondered. *Is she living in a parallel reality that involves Gavin?*

Has she found him there because of a connection they formed in previous lifetimes?

Those were definite possibilities, yet she was hardly an expert on the subject. She knew someone who was, however, and her first priority was to call him and ask his advice. They'd been friends in university and had even dated for a while. Her friend had gone on to study paranormal psychology, and although they hadn't kept in touch over the years, she'd followed his work with interest. Now she hoped and prayed that he could help solve the mysteries she'd uncovered. When she got through to him on the phone, she explained the situation in detail.

"This isn't as uncommon as you'd think, Adele," he responded. "You're absolutely right. A visit from this man could well be the impetus needed to draw her out of the coma."

"Do you know why she's choosing to remain there —if it *is* a choice—and what kinds of things she's experiencing?" Adele couldn't pass up the opportunity to learn more about a subject she found fascinating.

"Well," he explained, "we're eternal beings with an incredible ability to focus. It's through focus and intention that we create our reality. For the most part, we're not aware of it, but that reality is constantly shifting and changing; we're constantly recreating ourselves.

"I know this is in line with what you teach, but we've found that creation can take place across realms. And not just the physical and nonphysical," he clarified. "There appear to be layers of realms or realities that we experience. We hear them referred to as alternate or parallel realities, which hold the connotation of vertical experiences running side by side, occupying the same time, just different space. Only, time and space don't really exist; those are just measurements we've created to help define our experience here."

Her friend's knowledge enthralled her, and Adele continued to listen without interrupting.

"This is where it gets tricky." His enthusiasm was evident and Adele had to smile. It was obvious his heart was dedicated to solving the mysteries of the universe. "These planes overlap and intersect, creating distinctly unique yet connected realms. The part of us that's focused in a specific realm may be somewhat aware of what's going on in other realms, or not at all..." He paused for effect. "But our Higher Self is fully aware and simultaneously focused in these multiple realms, orchestrating the entire process effortlessly. I like to think of it as a complex playground for our Higher Selves, a place to experience contrast, determine preferences, and create with form and substance."

Adele needed to understand what he was saying. "So what Gavin through his dreams and Kathryn in her coma have experienced, then, is an overlapping of these realms. They've stepped into a realm where another part of them is living a different reality.

"I wonder, though, do they merge with their alternate selves and experience first hand, or do they merely observe?" She knew the answer before she'd finished speaking. "I'm sure they must be living it. The experience Gavin shared with me is too powerful to be just an observation."

"Right. As they focus in that realm, it becomes as real as any other, and they have the power to change it any way they want."

"You said this is common?"

"We experience it all the time. Sleep and even day-dreams draw us out of this realm temporarily, though we usually recall only bits and pieces. Comas, near-death experiences—anything traumatic—can cause us to escape into these other realms and experience them in a more profound way.

"It's possible to cross over consciously, too. Many people can attest to stepping into one of these other realms, merging as you say with their alternate selves in a deliberate way and having experiences, meeting people, and even bringing things back from these realms—like the picture Kathryn had. It's all just focus and energy movement."

They continued to talk, and Adele learned a great deal about a subject that had for so long mystified and intrigued her. She thanked her friend for his insights and his help, and promised to keep him updated on the situation. He'd not only shed a great deal of light on the subject, but he was able to give her the name of a government official, a close friend of his, who would have the power to grant Gavin a temporary pass.

GAVIN WENT HOME after dropping Adele off at her hotel, but he was barely aware of the drive. His mind was deep in thought. Kate was not only real, as he had already discovered, but she knew him and was now wanting, quite possibly needing, his help.

She knows me! Electricity surged through him. *She's been experiencing the same kinds of things I have. No wonder she feels so real to me.* He was elated at the idea of her being more than just a dream. She was a woman who had shared exhilarating and intimate adventures with him, someone he could now talk to about those memories—if indeed Adele was right and his presence in Kate's life would bring her back.

Adele seemed confident that she could arrange for him to see Kate. Gavin had no idea how, but he had to trust that the details would work themselves out. He didn't know how long it would take, either, and not knowing was the hardest part. Meanwhile, he needed to find a way to tell his family about her. He'd shared a little with his mom about a psychologist named Kathryn Harding, what he'd learned about her work on the Internet, and his desire to meet her. Now his mom deserved to hear the rest. He just hoped she wouldn't find it too strange.

He offered to help with lunch dishes the next day. That in itself wasn't unusual, but his mom must have sensed he wanted to talk, because she asked him what was on his mind.

"You know me too well," he teased, trying to be casual but feeling the tension in his stomach.

"You're easy to read," she smiled.

"Do you think it's possible," he began, "to connect with someone you've never met, never even talked to in person?"

"Maybe," she frowned. "I don't like to rule things out. Just because I don't know something doesn't mean it's not possible. Why do you ask?"

He told her about his experience in the infirmary, and she looked taken aback. Gavin hoped she wasn't offended that he hadn't shared it with her sooner.

"So that's what sparked your interest in this woman's work?"

"Yeah, that's what triggered it, but I think if I'd come across it any other way, I would have been just as intrigued by it. It's really helped me."

"I know it has, dear," she smiled. "From what you've told me, I can understand why. It's quite an amazing teaching. It's even challenged some of the things I believe and helped me to be more open minded."

"That's good," Gavin laughed uneasily, "because I just learned something that's pretty mind blowing. Kate was in a car accident right around the time I got sick. She's still in a coma—on life support."

"Oh, dear," Carol exclaimed.

"I met with a friend of hers yesterday. Her name is Adele. She…um…flew out here to talk to me." Gavin stopped to gauge his mom's reaction. "She told me that Kate's family wants to take her off life support, but Adele is convinced that Kate has been trying to communicate with her and…" he swallowed hard. "This is the really strange part…"

"Gavin, I've never seen you so nervous. What on earth is this about? You've always been able to talk to me. You know I won't judge you."

"Thanks," Gavin exhaled. "I really appreciate that. It's just...this is something I can't explain. It's...paranormal, and I didn't know what you'd think of that kind of thing."

"What do you mean by paranormal?"

"Mom, Kate knows me, too. I don't know how it's possible, but we're pretty sure that she's been having an experience similar to the one I had. Somehow we've connected and experienced things together on some level. The nurse heard her say my name, and Adele found a picture of me—of our family—among Kate's things. That's how she was able to track me down, and now she thinks that Kate is trying to communicate with us both. She wants me to go and see her...to see if it might..." Gavin's words trailed off as he noticed his mom's reaction.

She'd turned from the sink, and soapsuds were dripping on the floor. "But how on earth...?"

"That was the same reaction I had when Adele told me," he laughed again, hoping to break the tension. He really didn't want to mention his mom's handwriting on the back of the picture.

Carol wiped her hands on her apron and walked into the living room. Gavin followed with no idea what she was up to. She pulled a box from a cabinet and took it over to the sofa. "I had a dream," she explained. "It made no sense at the time, so I dismissed it, but now I wonder..."

"Wonder what?" Gavin asked as he watched her flip through loose photos in the box.

"A few weeks ago, I dreamed I was looking for that picture of all of us we had taken at your last birthday. Someone wanted to see it. I don't know who, but I remember searching for it."

She continued flipping through the pictures and then frowned as she looked up at her son. "It doesn't seem to be here. I wonder where else I could have put it. This is where I keep my photos till I get a chance to put them in an album. I got caught up over the winter, so I don't have many left in here."

A knowing seized Gavin as more pieces of the puzzle fell into place. Kate had acquired the picture so she could have Adele find it; he was sure of it. He was also confident that his mom's search would be futile.

"Did you actually see the picture?" Carol inquired. "Was it that one of the four of us...taken at the prison?"

Gavin nodded.

His mom was silent, and Gavin couldn't interpret her expression. He assumed she was trying to process the astounding things she'd just heard.

"So Kate's been trying to contact you," she stated calmly, indicating she'd fully accepted the strange set of circumstances.

"You're okay with this? I mean...it's so bizarre." Gavin was stunned at his mom's ability to accept it without question.

"God works in mysterious ways," she replied. "It's not for me to ask why."

Gavin suddenly had a déjà vu moment. He'd heard his mom use the common phrase often, but this time the words and the way she'd said them sounded familiar. Gavin was sure they'd had the same conversation before. It was eerie but powerful, and Gavin wondered what it meant.

Moving on, his mom began to speculate about how he'd get to see Kate. "You can't travel. They wouldn't make an exception, would they?"

"Adele thinks they might; she's working on it now."

"Gavin," Carol squeezed his arm, "I've learned to trust my feelings over the years. It's served me well. I have a feeling about this."

Gavin had heard his mom say those words many times before, too, but he had never fully understood the significance until that moment. "That's what Kate teaches!" he exclaimed. "That's our emotional guidance system. It's trusting how we feel and following what feels best.

"I feel it, too," he added. "I don't know how or why this all happened, but she's become an important part of my life. She's helped me so much, and now I want to help her...if I can."

Carol smiled lovingly, and Gavin could see the pride in her eyes. He gave her a hug and held her for a long moment. "I love you, Mom."

"I love you, too, son."

HAVING GOTTEN TO KNOW several of the nurses on Kathryn's ward, Adele was able to call and get regular updates on her friend's condition, which as of that morning had not changed. That link was comforting. She'd visited Kathryn every day, hoping her presence, her words, might have some effect. Now she hated being away from her but knew it was for the best; it was what Kathryn wanted.

The government official that her friend had suggested she call was away from his office on family business and couldn't be reached. Frustrated with the delay, Adele had no choice but to leave her name and number and wait for him to return her call. That left her with nothing but time on her hands and no reason not to return home—at least then she could be with Kathryn. She'd naively hoped that Gavin might accompany her back. Now it looked as though it would be several days, maybe longer, before she could talk to the man, not to mention the time it would take to secure Gavin's travel arrangements. The thought was disheartening.

Trusting her instincts, she decided to stay another day. She liked the idea of seeing Gavin again, of getting to know the man that Kathryn had formed such a deep connection with. She called to update him on her efforts, and he sounded pleased that she had the name of someone who could make things happen. He was eager to meet with her again, too.

As he picked her up at her hotel later that afternoon, she noted again how good looking he was and gave Kathryn a silent thumbs up for her taste in men. It was more than just his looks that made him a perfect match for Kathryn, however. He was kind and gentle and uncommonly wise for someone who hadn't had the benefit of formal training. His knowing seemed to come from a place of connectedness, not from books or lecture theaters.

As they visited, it was clear that he was keen to learn all he could about Kathryn. After answering several of his questions, however, Adele asked why he kept calling her Kate.

"That's how she introduced herself to me, to all of us, in her sessions at Swenton. I just assumed that's what everybody called her. I was surprised to hear you call her Kathryn; it sounds so formal."

"It feels that way, too," Adele admitted. "I've often thought Kate suited her better." She told him a little about Kathryn's past and the reason for the name change. "As trivial as the change seemed to others, it was her attempt to become someone new and deal with the traumas of her childhood."

"It's nice to learn more about her," Gavin smiled. "We talked so much about me in our sessions. There's something I've been wondering, though. She wore wedding rings, and I felt…kind of guilty, thinking about her the way I did. Afterward when I read about her late husband's work, I couldn't help but wonder… did she remarry? And if so, why doesn't her current husband have a say about what happens to her?"

"Kevin died four years ago," Adele informed him. "And no, she's never remarried. She's never even looked at another man as far as I know. I'm surprised that her rings would be a part of your experience with her. It must represent something. People tried to persuade her to date again. I even encouraged it after a while, and it became a sensitive issue between us. I knew how much she loved Kevin, but I also saw how lonely and withdrawn she was becoming. She finally took off the rings just over a year ago, but it was a hard decision for her."

"Sounds like she's had more than her share of pain."

"Definitely more than some, but it's made her who she is. Kathryn's the most giving, caring person I've ever known. I miss her so much…" Adele felt the dam burst. She'd tried to be strong for so long, to be there for her friend and stay positive, but with Gavin she felt she could be vulnerable. It was obvious that he loved Kathryn, too.

Gavin offered her a comforting hug, and Adele appreciated the gesture. He was choked up, too, and she felt a kinship with him. She could finally share her heart with someone who understood the pain, loss, and helplessness she'd been feeling for weeks.

"She'll come back to us," Gavin tried to assure her. "I can't believe all this has happened for nothing. There's got to be a greater purpose."

"I believe that, too," she sniffed, digging in her purse for a tissue. "I'm so glad I met you, Gavin McDermott."

Chapter 24

Gavin spent the next few days searching the Internet, trying to learn more about the supernatural events that were happening in both his life and Kate's. Part of it was natural curiosity, just wanting answers, but more than anything he wanted to keep busy and keep his mind occupied as he waited, again, for a verdict from someone who held the power to greatly influence his future.

His nights were filled with confusing dreams. Some were faded reproductions of past adventures with Kate, while others were random bits of information coming at him—a word, a thought, a face, an idea—with no apparent reason, at least none that he could figure out. He tried to make sense of it based on the understanding he'd received from Kate and the information he'd gathered since.

As he lay in bed one evening, he attempted to sum it up in his mind. *I know I'm connected to something greater; I'm part of a system that perfectly supports me.* The thought reminded him of advice he'd received when he first went to Swenton: "It's a system, kid. You learn the system and you'll do just fine."

Life is a system, too, he concluded. *A set of seemingly random parts that make up the whole. But those parts aren't separate at all; everything is interconnected and acting in a unified way. And I'm an important component in this system.*

He reminded himself of the life-changing truths he'd learned from Kate. *My thoughts are creating my reality, and I have the ability to change those thoughts.* He'd experienced it more than once, and it gave him a sense of power as never before. It was the very power he'd been so desperately seeking as a teenager.

And reality...it's not some immovable, unchangeable set of circumstances. It's a constantly moving, constantly changing, fluid set of observances controlled solely by my focus.

So how does all this apply to Kate and her current situation? he asked the Source of greater knowing he'd come to trust. *She's part of something bigger, too. She's creating her own reality just like I am. She isn't just a victim of some drunk driver. Her ability to choose hasn't been taken away just because she's lying unconscious in that hospital bed.* He shook his head. *It can't be; it doesn't fit with everything I know and believe—everything she teaches.* Gavin continued to sort through the knowledge he'd collected and apply it as best he could to the situation.

At some point he drifted into a fitful sleep, knowing yet questioning, seeking and finding yet driven to seek more.

ADELE WATCHED her friend. Kathryn's face was pale and her body so still it seemed she'd vacated it altogether. The machines by her bed regulated her breathing and fed her, but the Kathryn she loved had gone somewhere else completely. Adele longed to know where and most importantly why.

"Kathryn," she said softly as she took her friend's hand. "Sweetie, I'm going to call you Kate now, because I think that's who you are deep down inside. Kate, I have great news. I met Gavin. I talked to him. He's wonderful."

At the mention of Gavin's name, Kate's hand twitched. Adele felt it, and her pulse quickened with excitement. "I found him, sweetie! The clues you left—they led me right to him. And Kate," she added emphatically, "he knows you too. He's dreamed about you. Gavin wants to come and see you!"

Adele felt the movement again. It was slight, almost indiscernible, like a muscle twitching, but the fact that it moved in response to Gavin's name had to mean something. The nurse entered the room, and Adele shared the exciting news. "Her hand—I felt a slight movement!"

The nurse smiled sympathetically. "Don't get your hopes up, honey; it's pretty common. I've felt it, too, when I'm bathing her, or changing her. I'm sorry." She touched Adele's arm. "I know how hard this is. I had a sister in the same condition. We held out hope for so long, but…" The nurse shook her head.

Adele refused to be swayed. She didn't want to hear about the cases that didn't make it. What she wanted was evidence to support her belief that Kate would be okay. After the nurse left, Adele resumed the conversation, telling Kate everything about her visit with Gavin. Even after she'd told her friend all she could remember of their conversations, she continued to talk, frequently mentioning his name in the hope that Kate's hand might twitch again, but nothing happened.

"He's easy on the eyes, Kate," she tried to joke while holding back tears. "I knew you had it in you. Didn't I tell you you'd meet someone great?"

She yearned to feel the movement again, to know for sure that Kate was trying to communicate with her, but she was struggling with her own doubts. "Gavin loves you, Kate," Adele said, crying now. "He wants to see you. Wake up, Kate," she begged. "Please wake up."

GAVIN AND HIS DAD were finishing a project, and Gavin had to go into town for supplies. They had several orders for furniture, now, and the potential for a lucrative business. He'd been to Redding numerous times since his release from prison, and he often ran into people he knew. Although polite, they seemed uncomfortable around him. Older folks kept the conversation to his parents, farming, or the weather. People his age offered inconsequential gossip about mutual acquaintances. Gavin wondered if he would ever be just a regular guy in his hometown or if he'd always be the one that people smiled at but talked about behind his back.

He usually kept his trips brief, getting what he needed and returning straight home, but this time felt the desire to drive around. He'd been avoiding the area of town where the murder had taken place, but now part of him needed to see it again, needed to confront it. His heart rate accelerated as he turned down the street leading to the old mill.

The town's lumber mill, having shut down, had been a hangout for young people when Gavin was a teenager. Now the old buildings were gone, completely, and row housing lined the street. Even those were looking run down.

Although the landscape had changed, a certain essence remained. It was no doubt linked to the neighborhood's sordid past. Junk littered the front yards, broken-down cars were parked on the street, and many of the houses were in need of repair. Several young children were playing in the street, and Gavin slowed to a crawl as he approached, hoping they would move out of the way quickly so he could pass by.

As he waited, he noticed a young man walking toward him. Gavin took a second glance, and stiffened at what he saw. Looking back at him was Ryan, the kid he'd met in prison. To be more accurate, he was the kid he'd met in his dream, and now he was walking toward him on a street in Redding. Gavin wanted nothing more than to speed away from what he was sure was an apparition, but he couldn't move. Two of the children had left the street, but the littlest one was still playing, totally oblivious to traffic or the fact that his mother was yelling at him from a nearby porch.

Ryan approached the passenger side of his vehicle, and Gavin reluctantly opened the window part way. "Hi Gavin," the young man smiled. "Feels pretty good to be free, doesn't it?"

"But you…" Gavin stammered. "I saw you in the infirmary. You...died."

"I told you nothing's real," Ryan replied. "You created your experience there. You even created me."

"Who are you?" Gavin demanded, feeling frightened. He had no idea what kind of strange magic he was caught up in, but it was beginning to get too weird.

"I'm part of you; I'm here to help you remember."

Something about the familiar words caused Gavin to relax slightly.

"It's okay. I told you you'd understand, and you will. Just believe. Remember what I said to you that day in the shop?"

Gavin closed his eyes, and Ryan's words echoed in his mind: "You could be anywhere you want, tell any story you want. But you get stuck sometimes, believing you can't leave. The prison is really in your mind."

When he opened his eyes, Ryan was walking away. "What does that mean?" Gavin called after him. "I'm not in prison anymore.

"What does it mean?" Gavin called even louder, but Ryan didn't answer.

ADELE HAD SPENT HOURS on the phone trying to reach the man who could authorize Gavin's release. He was back in his office, and she'd finally gotten through to his personal assistant, letting her know it was an urgent matter. Now Adele was waiting to hear from him, but it had been days, and time was running out.

Kate's father and sister showed up at the hospital that evening as Adele sat with Kate. Adele shared her belief in Kate's well-being, told them about the movement she'd felt as she held Kate's hand, and even relayed the possibility of an "old friend" coming to visit, but they weren't swayed. They were more determined than ever to help Kate find her peace, and announced their decision to have the machines turned off the following day.

Adele's tears failed to move them. They were heartless, uncaring murderers in her eyes, and she seethed in anger as she left the hospital. *Oh God, help me*, she cried, nearly out of her mind with the thoughts that were threatening to overwhelm her. At home she wept until she had no more tears and then sat exhausted, feeling as powerless as she ever had in her life.

As she wiped away the last of the tears, she asked herself what advice Kate would have for her. Adele was immediately aware that she was allowing her thoughts to run unchecked; she was completely at their mercy. In her practice she had an array of tools and techniques she used in helping others, and she suddenly realized that those tools were available to her as well. She believed in their effectiveness. She'd seen countless lives transformed by them, yet for some reason wasn't using them herself—and she desperately needed the comfort they could bring her.

Her inner space had been sadly neglected, and she longed to revisit it. After spending a few minutes meditating and consciously releasing thoughts that had been bombarding her, she slowly began to recognize the sanctuary she'd created. Being there was soothing and exactly what she needed. She'd been carrying the entire weight of the situation on her shoulders, and to be free of it, if only for a moment, was blissful relief.

The next step was to identify the emotions she was feeling and reclaim the power she'd given them. With a little effort she managed to accomplish it, and the wave that washed over her was powerful.

Adele spent some time reminding herself of the truths she had come to know and believe—truths that Kate held sacred as well. She then deliberately moved up the emotional scale, letting anger serve its purpose as she thought again about Kate's self-serving family. Moving past anger, she found a measure of relief in frustration and overwhelment$_4$ before she finally caught a whiff of hope.

And hope felt euphoric! Compared to the depths from which she'd just emerged, she may as well have found eternal bliss. It was the movement itself, not the distance, that was the distinguishing factor, she realized. Moving into vibrational alignment with who she really was, was something she'd never tire of.

Hope allowed her to think of Kate and trust that a miracle could still happen. It reminded her that Gavin was in the picture now, and that there had to be a reason for the situation unfolding as it had. Hope also reminded her that her dear friend, though lying in a coma, was still creating her own reality, and nothing could happen that wasn't of her own creation.

"GAVIN, HONEY, WAKE UP." Carol jostled his shoulder. "You're dreaming."

"Mom?" Gavin opened his eyes to familiar surroundings and his mother leaning over his bed.

"I heard you call out. Did you have a nightmare?"

Gavin sighed in relief. Ryan had been just a dream. He took a few minutes to focus before answering her. "I…I think I just got a message."

"From Kate?" Carol asked, as if receiving messages in that manner was now commonplace.

"No, from Ryan." Gavin had already told his mom about the young man. "He reminded me of something he said in prison, but I don't know what it means." He relayed Ryan's words.

"That's interesting. The prison is in your mind." She paused, contemplating the words. "That's in line with what Kate teaches about creating your own reality."

"Kate!" Gavin looked at his mom with sudden awareness. "This is about Kate now! She's in a prison of sorts. She created her experience…maybe she needs to be reminded that she can leave anytime she wants."

"Do you really think it's that simple?"

"Yes!" Gavin was sure he'd received the answer Kate needed. "If I could just remind her of that, maybe she'd find the power to come back."

"Gavin, you and Kate have a powerful connection. You've talked to each other in a way that's beyond my understanding. Maybe you could still reach her somehow…with your mind."

"Maybe."

After Carol left, he replayed Ryan's message. He could still see the boy's face clearly. Though merely a character in his dreamworld, the kid had profoundly impacted Gavin's life, answering some of his deepest questions. Now in his own unique way the kid had helped him see Kate's situation clearly. Gavin offered a silent thank-you, both to the messenger and for the message he believed Kate needed to hear.

If only I could talk to her, he sighed. *She needs to hear this.*

He considered his mom's suggestion. For some reason, Gavin hadn't thought about trying to communicate with Kate in that way. Adele believed he could make a difference by being with Kate in person, and he'd been thinking from that perspective too. His mom was absolutely right. He and Kate had rendezvoused in another realm, and she was still there. That's where he needed to reach her.

ADELE GOT UP EARLY to go to the hospital. She wanted to spend time with Kate, talk to her, entice her to come back, but she was no longer feeling desperate. She'd found peace and whatever the outcome, she could always reclaim that.

Instead of pulling up a chair as she usually did, Adele sat on the edge of the bed, wanting to be as close as she could. She took Kate's hand in both of hers, holding it tight. "Kate," she began. "I love you, sweetie. I'm truly honored to be your friend. I've learned so much from you. I owe you so much…" Adele took a deep breath as she attempted to hold back her tears.

"Whatever happens today..." she continued with difficulty, "I believe you're the one orchestrating it. But sweetie...I just have to say that if it's possible, somehow..." she cried, "please come back. There's so much you wanted to do with your life yet. And Gavin…" As she said the name, Adele felt the twitch again.

"Gavin loves you, sweetie. He's your soul mate. He couldn't be here, but he wanted to be. He wanted to be with you. If you just...wake up, you can be with him. You can be...together." Adele couldn't continue; the tears had their way, and she spent a few minutes weeping. They weren't so much tears of sorrow as acknowledgment and appreciation for the dear friend Kathryn Harding had been to her.

"I was able to apply what we teach, Kate," Adele sniffed, lovingly rubbing her friend's hand. "I was having trouble for a little while. I was angry and sad…but this works; it's such a powerful method. I found peace.

I know it's going to be okay now. I have your love and your friendship and your amazing teaching, and they'll always be mine to treasure." She brought Kate's hand to her lips and held it there as hot tears trickled onto the lily-white skin. "I love you, sweetie. I'll always love you."

Adele left the hospital before Kate's family arrived. She couldn't bear to be present when the machines were turned off. She wanted to find her peaceful inner place again and spend time there with cherished memories of her beloved friend.

GAVIN'S HOPES VANISHED as he heard the discouraging news. Adele had just informed him that Kate's life support would be removed in less than an hour. She'd been to visit her one last time, and as she apologized for not being able to arrange for him to see Kate, Adele sounded somber. Still, she managed to offer encouraging words. She'd found her power, she said, and now she was able to think of Kate in a loving, positive way. It would be her final gift to her friend and mentor. Gavin admired her strength as he thanked her for all that she had done.

He felt numb when the conversation ended. He desperately wanted to reach out to Kate, to offer her one final lifeline to grasp, but he wasn't sure he could do it. For the past few days he'd been trying unsuccessfully to hold her image in his mind, reach out to her, feel her soft skin and her silky hair. The problem was, he was keenly aware that the images and the sensations were fabricated; they didn't come to him as easily or as naturally as they had in the past. He tried again, this time with renewed determination to find her wherever she was.

Kate, it's Gavin. I know it's been a while since we've had one of our adventures, but I thought maybe you'd like to...you know...go sailing, or maybe flying. You love to fly, Kate. You look so beautiful with the wind in your hair. Fly with me, Kate...one more time, he begged.

With eyes closed, he imagined taking her hand, stroking her skin. He tried to recall the rich texture of her voice as she led him in a guided meditation.

He was struggling to concentrate—thoughts of losing her were moving in quickly—but with tenacity he continued, allowing the love he felt for her to fuel one final attempt.

Letting his body relax completely, he envisioned strong air currents lifting him, and he tried to feel the dips and dives as he became one with the flow. He concentrated hard, creating hills and trees below, even houses and farms. With beauty all around him, he focused on the feeling of air rushing past as he navigated the skies.

Then it happened. The scenery came to life, drawing him in. Effortlessly he soared higher, taking in the panoramic view. The weather was idyllic with the sun warm on his face and the breeze slight. Below him was a lake, and in the center a small sailboat drifted lazily. As he focused on it, he was instantly drawn into the boat and found himself staring at Kate. Sitting relaxed in the bow, her arms were draped back and her long legs extended just as he'd seen her many times before. She looked at him with an expression he couldn't interpret.

As in his dreams, it felt good just to sit and watch her. It had been so long since he'd felt her presence, and he reveled in it now. They were together. Gazing at her lovely face, he couldn't keep from telling her how he felt. *I love you, Kate. I've been wanting to tell you that for a long time.*

"I know," she replied, showing no trace of emotion.

I remembered something, Kate, he said quickly, trying to disregard her apathy. *When I was in prison, I learned that I was creating my experience there. I was free to leave, yet I couldn't because it was my mind that held me there; it was my beliefs.*

Kate frowned at his words.

Gavin felt a chill as the wind suddenly picked up causing heavy clouds to block out the sun. He had to speak louder to be heard over the howling gale. *Kate, I think this applies to you too. Your beliefs are holding you somewhere you don't want to be.*

The boat began pitching back and forth with the power of the waves, and cold pellets of rain battered his cheek. Gavin moved closer to Kate, nearly yelling now. *You can leave any time you like. You're free. Nothing is holding you here.*

Kate looked at him with a slight longing, then shook her head in disagreement. All of a sudden the boat lurched and tipped sideways, throwing them from their seats.

"Gavin!" she cried.

He reached for Kate, and they were both tossed overboard. He felt them moving through the air as the storm's fury propelled them. Holding her close, Gavin understood that what he was experiencing was a creation of his consciousness, and he wasn't afraid; all he could think of was how incredible it felt to hold her in his arms.

"Gavin..." she cried again. This time water muffled her cry as they plunged beneath the waves.

It's not real, Kate. Gavin repeated the words she'd once said to him. *You can change it with your thoughts.* He tried to hold her, but she slipped from his arms as the waves tossed them about.

It's not real! he called as the waves pulled her away. *Kate!*

It does not matter where you are; where you are is shifting constantly...you must turn your attention to where you want to go.

—ABRAHAM-HICKS

Chapter 25

Kate felt Gavin's arms around her; she heard his words, but she was confused. The words sounded familiar, and she knew they were what she needed to hear, but she felt powerless to act. They continued to echo in her mind as she felt herself slipping away— away from Gavin and from all that was familiar.

Suddenly she found herself standing at a crossroads. She looked in one direction and saw the sun shining brilliantly. Everything within its magnificent radiance glimmered like gold. It was warm on her skin, and it illuminated the lush landscape. Trees were ripe with delicious-looking fruit. Gentle animals basked in the warmth beside a tranquil stream, and waterfalls cascaded down picturesque hills in the distance. It was idyllic; it was a more splendid paradise than she had ever dared imagine, and she turned toward it.

Curious, she looked over her shoulder to see what was in the other direction. A narrow dirt road carved its way through a thick forest. The road was cast in shadows, even complete darkness in spots. In the distance a light twinkled. At first Kate barely noticed it, but as she continued to look, the light became brighter and more distinct. It was flickering and dancing, teasing almost.

She stood at the crossroads for a moment longer and realized that she had a choice. She could choose the magnificent paradise, or she could follow the road with the alluring light. She could have the assurance of comfort and luxury and bliss, or she could opt for the enticing adventure that the flickering light seemed to offer. There was no right or wrong, no good or bad, no reward or punishment; it was simply a matter of preference. Moreover, she sensed that the paradise would be waiting for her return, should she choose the adventure.

Kate made her choice; she turned toward the flickering light and began to walk. As she did, the landscape opened up. It became familiar, and she saw people and places that she recognized. But it was the light that continued to entice her. She was curious now; it felt so compelling.

Memories began to move to the forefront of her mind. She thought of her dear friend, Adele, and smiled as she remembered the good times they'd had, the work they'd done together. She was proud of their accomplishments. It made her realize how much she loved her work, loved helping people. She realized, too, that there was much more she wanted to do.

As she drew closer to the light, another memory surfaced. This one wasn't as clear, but as she focused on it, details began to emerge. She saw herself working in a prison and felt the satisfaction of seeing lives transformed.

Then she remembered.

Looking into the distance, she saw him. He had a smile on his face as he watched her. Her heart filled with joy as she realized that her choice included Gavin. He was the light. He was the path that she'd chosen. She hurried toward him.

Her pulse began to quicken as she ran. She felt her body come alive with the forward movement. She'd made her decision, and she couldn't wait to experience the adventure that it held.

Love is the only reality and it is not a mere sentiment. It is the ultimate truth that lies at the heart of creation.

—RABINDRANATH TAGORE

Chapter 26

Adele walked into the hospital room and embraced her friend. She was reduced to tears each time she saw her; Kate's smiling face was a joy to behold. She'd heard the story several times now, and each time, Kate would remember another detail and add to the overall picture. The miracle that Adele had hoped and prayed for—and believed in the possibility of—had manifested. Kate had come back, quite literally, from the dead.

She hadn't been there when they'd turned off the machines that were keeping Kate alive, but from her apartment, Adele had the most compelling urge to go back to the hospital. She listened to her guidance without questioning and arrived to find Kate not only alive but awake and well. With the machines no longer performing her body's necessary functions, Kate had clinically died and remained that way for a few minutes before the monitors began to detect a slight pulse. It strengthened on its own, and within several minutes, to the complete shock of her family, she had regained consciousness.

Kate and Adele had talked for many hours about the strange phenomena that occurred while she was unconscious, and Kate was aware that Gavin not only knew of her but had shared a similar experience.

"Tell me again what he's like," Kate begged. She was eager to meet Gavin but admitted that, given the circumstances, talking to him on the phone might be awkward, so she'd opted to be patient and let the details of their 'first' meeting take care of themselves.

Adele laughed. "From what you've told me, he's just like what you imagined. And why shouldn't he be? You created him."

"I can't believe he feels the same way," Kate shook her head. "It's like having the most wonderful dream and then waking up to find that it's true."

"That's exactly what it's like," Adele concurred, still in awe of the extraordinary unfolding of events. She'd spent many hours drawing her own conclusions and had discussed the matter further with her friend in paranormal psychology. Having talked with Kate and Gavin about their dreams, Adele questioned why their experiences differed slightly. If they had actually rendezvoused in another realm, she couldn't understand why their memories of it wouldn't be the same.

The reasons, her friend explained, involved perspective and recall. He said that everyone's experience was influenced by their personal perspective, their beliefs, and their thoughts. A person's desires played a significant role as well. And what people remembered from their trips to other realities varied considerably.

He likened it to the *Holodeck* on Star Trek: The Next Generation. Characters could step into the simulation facility, set criteria for the adventure they wanted to have, and the result would be a virtual reality experience of their own making. Others would obviously be part of the simulated environment, but their perspective would vary, and their ability to recall the experience would depend on many different factors.

Adele understood now that Kate and Gavin, having played together in past lifetimes, chose to include each other in their current adventures. They'd escaped into another realm and enjoyed each other's presence from their unique perspectives. It would be fun for them to compare their experiences as they began their relationship in the physical realm.

She'd yet to share her newfound knowledge with Kate; she knew they'd have many satisfying discussions in the weeks to come, but for now there was something more pressing that Adele wanted to ask. "Kate, do you know what made the difference? Was it that you couldn't come back sooner, or that you didn't know how? Or were you having so much fun you didn't want to?" she added jokingly.

"I'm not sure," Kate responded. "I know for a while I truly enjoyed it there. I could experience and accomplish things I'd only dreamed of here. After a while, I think I wanted to come back, but for whatever reason I was stuck. It felt that way, anyway."

"But didn't you know all that you'd learned here?"

"It's funny. I did at the beginning, but it's kind of like our experience here. We arrive knowing everything but get so immersed in our environment that we forget and have to learn it again. Even there, I was aware that a greater part of me was focused elsewhere. I trusted that greater knowing for the most part, but there were times, especially at the end when I felt I was drowning, that I forgot to trust."

"Gavin said he was with you!" Adele blurted, suddenly remembering the juicy tidbit she'd wanted to share. Then, noticing the surprised look on Kate's face, she explained, "When I called to tell him you were all right, we talked awhile. He said that he was trying to reach you in his mind..." Adele relayed the story Gavin had shared with her. "He was holding you, and he felt you slip away."

"I felt it, too!" Kate exclaimed. "And I heard his voice. He was trying to tell me it wasn't real. Oh my God, I just remembered that now!

"Right after that I saw my choices. I think..." She looked pensively at Adele. "Maybe I'd already died, according to the machines anyway, and it was in that brief moment I made my decision."

The details of Kate's experience fascinated Adele. "Was it an easy decision, then, to come back?"

"I could have gone either way. There's really no such thing as death, by the way; it's just a change of focus. All

I know is that I felt completely at peace. Both choices appealed to me. Paradise was breathtakingly beautiful, yet something about it was familiar, like I'd been there before, and I knew I'd see it again. I honestly didn't know what the other road held for me. I had no memory of it in that moment, yet it was too enticing to pass up."

"I'm so glad you made this choice," Adele smiled. "It's not always paradise here, but it can be a pretty exciting adventure."

A knock on the door caused them to turn toward the sound. Standing in the opening was the very one they had been discussing. Both women were shocked. Kate for obvious reasons, and Adele because she'd been expecting Gavin's call. Knowing that he would be arriving sometime that day, she'd been planning to meet him at the airport. She'd also intended to prepare Kate with a couple hours notice.

Nobody moved for several long seconds. Introductions weren't necessary, yet Adele searched for something appropriate to say.

"Oh my God!" Kate's hands flew to her mouth. "Gavin!"

"Hi, Kate," he smiled.

Adele could sense Gavin's nervousness as he walked into the room. She turned to Kate, whose shocked expression was still evident, even as a smile slowly formed on her face. "I'm sorry I didn't tell you, sweetie. I've been working on getting Gavin's travel restrictions lifted. I found someone who could pull strings, but I didn't want to say anything. I had no idea how long it would take. The approval just went through this morning. I was going to prepare you...."

"Please," Kate insisted, "don't apologize. I...it's just..." she started to laugh, but tears weren't far away. "I don't know what to say." She looked at Gavin and began to cry.

He went to her without hesitation. Kate reached out to him as he approached her bed, and the two simply looked at each other, unspoken love radiating from their eyes.

Adele watched the heartwarming scene and had to wipe away a tear of her own. "Well," she cleared her throat. "I'm going to give you two some time to...um," she laughed, "get re-acquainted."

As she turned to leave, Gavin touched her arm. He was obviously having a hard time with his emotions, but his eyes told her what was in his heart.

"Thank you," he managed to say.

Walking toward the door, Adele turned back to see her dear friend held tightly in the arms of the man she loved.

Hmmm, she smiled happily as she thought of all that had transpired. *This is the perfect end to an amazing story,* she mused. *Kate loved and lost...and now love is hers again. She lived and died...and now she gets to experience the fullness of life once more.*

*And Gavin...*she continued. *he chose years of bondage just so he could know true freedom...and through it he found his soul mate.*

Love is such a powerful force. It reached through time and space to unite these two beautiful souls. Adele was honored to have witnessed that power, and to have played a small part in bringing Kate and Gavin together. *It's such a satisfying ending, yet so much is just beginning. They're together; their relationship is finally real, and yet…*

Reality… she shook her head, laughing, as she went to the hospital cafeteria to get a cup of coffee. *I'm beginning to think it's seriously overrated.*

~The End~

Notes

1. www.robertscheinfeld.com

2. The process called the "Power Transfer" in this book is based on the teaching of Robert Scheinfeld in his book, *Busting Loose From the Money Game* (Hoboken, NJ: John Wiley & Sons, 2006) p. 103

3. The principles of Law of Attraction mentioned in this book—including the process called "Moving up the Emotional Scale"—are based on the teaching of Abraham-Hicks. www.abraham-hicks.com. "Moving up the Emotional Scale" is described in detail in their book, *Ask and It Is Given, Learning to Manifest Your Desires* (Carlsbad, CA: Hay House, 2004) p. 293

4. A word coined by Abraham and used in the teaching/ writing of Abraham-Hicks.

CPSIA information can be obtained at www.ICGtesting.com
Printed in the USA
LVOW060816070512

280567LV00001B/2/P